The
DOOMSDAY GROUP

The
DOOMSDAY GROUP

Jean Seitter Cummins

FRANKLIN MILLS PRESS

Franklin Mills Press
P.O. Box 906
Kent, Ohio 44240

ISBN 1-885663-04-8

www.doomsdaygroup.com

Printed in the United States of America by:
    McNaughton & Gunn
    960 Woodland Drive
    Saline, Michigan 48176

Cover art by Sequoia Brown

Typesetting and design by:
    Sans Serif Inc.
    203 West Michigan Avenue, Suite 201
    Saline, Michigan 48176

For my parents,
Maurice and Florence Seitter
"Wish you were here."

ONE

Christian Wahrmutter's eyes scanned the lines of code while his mind battled the uneasy feeling that he had done all this before. Characters danced in front of his eyes, appeared and disappeared, weaving in and out of columns, elusive as smoke. Like tracks, he thought to himself, pressing his fingertips hard against his forehead, enjoying the pressure, willing it to distract him. Like clues, he decided licking his lips, to a mystery he would never solve, not while his head beat like this and the taste of a hangover lingered in his mouth.

Tess had done it again, another long dinner followed by brandy in the Queen Anne chairs in front of the fire. It wasn't the brandy, though, not the Courvoisier that Tess always served. It must have been the Merlot, some cheap Chilean stuff he had picked up at the grocery store. Deep and fruity and laced with God knows what chemicals, and him so tired after a day spent in front of the dancing lines of code, chasing the mystery. He could see Tess's arms, long and amazingly white, emerging from her caftan, holding the bottle effortlessly, the way she did everything, pouring glass after glass with the Moonstone ring glinting on her finger.

It always seemed like such a good idea, an evening with his mother, a hearty meal and the chance to do his laundry. Except the laundry never got done and the conversation always went to his head more quickly even than the wine and the shifting depths of the fire. Then waking up the next morning with the fire gone cold and an afghan pulled up over his shoulders and the taste of loathing in his mouth. He had done it again. Why did her charm and her conversation still take him unawares. He had a place to be every morning and a job that wouldn't wait.

You work too hard, she chided him, padding out in her bare feet to brew a pot of strong tea and make him some toast. When he was little she had never done that. He had made his way alone through the empty wine bottles and overflowing ash trays, the stew pot hardening unwashed in the sink. He remembered making a breakfast of cheese and crackers still lying on the tray from the night before. And fruit, there was always fruit in the bowl on the center of the table. It was a mother's duty to always keep fresh fruit in the house.

Getting up with her son, fixing his breakfast, checking to see that his clothes were clean and that they matched, helping him remember his lunch and his homework, that was someone else's job. Those mothers on television, the Brady Bunch and the Partridge Family, they did that. Tess laughed at him for loving those shows so much. But sometimes they watched together, those nights when no one came over, side by side on the couch, wrapped up in an old comforter. Christian remembered the feel of those long arms wrapped around him and the smell of cigarettes on her breath.

"Where's your life, Christian?" she asked him now, fussing over him, brushing an imaginary speck from his shoulder. "And where did you get those clothes? You look like a crew member on the Enterprise. Like those men—" her hands paused dramatically in midair—"who are they, you know, those Japanese who climb up the sides of buildings?"

"Ninjas," he said reaching in front of her to get the toast before it burned, smiling in spite of himself. "Corporate Ninjas, we dress in black to blend in, so we can take our enemies unaware."

"That's right," she raised her arms in a stretch and he could see that she was still wearing her bracelets from the night before. "And you can climb right up the sides of buildings."

"Like a commando, a master of stealth," he spread his toast with imported marmalade. No grape jelly here, only the best, no matter what it cost.

"Like an ant," she corrected him, yawning. "Don't forget to lock up when you leave." Maternal duty done, she padded back to bed where she would no doubt remain until noon.

Christian forced his eyes back to the code. They should have programs to do this, he thought, programs to search out the tell-tale strings and insert new code. And of course they did have programs but most of them were customized to a particular application. So many places to hide a date and so many different consequences ranging from none at all to crashing the program, not to mention the planet if all the programs on all the computers that ran our world blew up at once. Christian glanced out of the window in the big industrial loft where The Doomsday Group had its offices. It was a typical midwestern winter day. The horizon so low he was sure that he could reach up and touch it. The smokestack across the river belching ugly black smoke against what was left of the sky.

The urge for a cigarette flared up as brief and intense as a match. Christian snuffed it out. Some people thought that the pollution would kill us or maybe we could kill ourselves with cigarettes and fast food. But Christian knew better. It was the computers that would get us in the end. Our world would end with something as insignificant as a date buried by a guy who didn't like his job, a guy like him maybe, looking out the window at that same smoke, longing for a cigarette, saying "screw it!" Jamming it in anywhere, where it made no sense, where not even Christian could find it, saying screw it and going out for a cigarette.

It was this carelessness that gave Christian a mission, gave him a job as a COBOL programmer, hunting for the tell-tale strings and analyzing their significance. The job that no computer could do or none that the Doomsday Group and its clients could afford, anyway. Hunt for the code that told the computer each two digit YY was equal to 19YY, determine if it had anything to do with the operation or if it was there because some early chiphead was obsessed with dates. If it was worth fixing, insert a new string to read each YY over 50 as 19YY and each one under 50 as 20YY. That was one fix anyway, the one favored by his employers because it was easy to explain to people with no brains, like their clients and most of their staff.

The fact that human judgment was required to analyze the effects of each string did not trouble the founders of The Doomsday Group. They were not in it for the long haul. This was the full employment solution and it was good for another 40 years or so. Then some poor son of a bitch could go back in and redo it all. Christian's son maybe or his grandson if he hurried.

The twitchy little blonde in front of him was still on the phone. Something about her son and how long he could stay wherever he was and when somebody named Junior was coming home . . . and damn! He threw down his pen. No wonder he thought he had seen all this before. His concentration was shot. Between his hangover and her baby sitter, he was never going to get any work done! He jammed the printout into a drawer. Too loud! He hadn't meant to be so loud.

The blonde turned startled, a deer in the headlights. Her eyes were big and wide, her face as vacant as he had imagined. She had probably been a COBOL programmer for all of 15 minutes. He could tell by the way she cradled the receiver—as though she were hiding it—that she had been warned. Too many phone calls, too much noise. She put her hand over the mouthpiece. "I'm sorry," she whispered, "it's my son. He's sick and I—yes, I'm still here," she turned back to the telephone. "Tell Junior that I'm paying you . . . extra! That's why he's there so late."

She reached for her purse, a big cheap carryall, spilling out with odds and ends, a bottle of water, a hairbrush, extra shoes and what looked like a rubber dinosaur. My god, it was. Stegosaurus sitting right in her purse, guarding her keys. She rooted frantically in all the debris for something—her wallet? No, she pushed the wallet aside, still murmuring sympathetically into the receiver and pulled out—of course—her checkbook. He bet it was out of balance, a long line of debits trailing to the left, the balance never carried forward from the previous page.

She closed her eyes. He could see her counting frantically on her fingers. "One hundred and twenty, this afternoon, I promise. I know, no checks! I'll stop by the machine on my way home. Okay, at lunch, I'll do it at lunch. Junior likes the kids to be gone when he gets home. I know, I don't blame him. But wait . . ." There was a long dramatic pause. Christian gave up pretending he wasn't listening. "Eighty five would be almost as good, right? Well then, don't tell him. Just until Friday. You know I'm good for it. Thanks, you're an angel." She put the receiver down carefully and stopped a minute to catch her breath. When she looked up, Christian was still staring. It didn't seem to bother her. "She loves Della Reese," she confided easily.

He liked the way she smiled.

"Of course I shouldn't be doing this," she told him in the elevator. They were on their way downstairs for a cup of cappuccino. My treat, he had assured her when she hesitated. "I've been on the phone all morning. I tried to get my family to take care of him. So he could stay home. He has a temperature."

Christian nodded. He remembered. Her mother, it had sounded like, and a sister or maybe a cousin and somebody named Auntie Lala.

"I've been warned." Her head was down now and he couldn't see her face. "About all the phone calls. He warned me this morning."

"He" was of course their manager, Slater. "Just going down for some coffee." Christian had called out as they passed his desk. "She has some questions about the code." And when he frowned. "Nothing for you to worry about. But it will be easier to talk downstairs—without disturbing the others?" Bingo! Slater nodded wisely. He was wearing dark green pants and a matching collarless shirt. Today might also be a silk blazer day. No. The double breasted vest, like an old waistcoast, with just the hint of a collar, hung over the back of his chair, ready to be assumed, the minute the phone rang and Slater was called in to an executive meeting.

What were those meetings about, Christian mused idly. Not about the work. Slater didn't know anything about the work. Maybe they were coordinating their accessories.

"It'll be all right, though. If you meant what you said . . ?"

"What?" Christian snapped to attention. "Oh, you mean about the code. Sure, we can talk about the code." The elevator opened to the first floor. He touched her arm lightly, guiding her toward the coffee stand, realizing too late that it was a gesture of unwarranted familiarity, one that she might resent in a coworker. "How would you like it?" Tess had demanded. "Strangers grabbing your arm and patting your back and telling you to smile?"

Christian flushed at the memory. He was about to withdraw his hand, when she looked up and smiled. As though she liked the fact that he wanted to guide her, as though she were looking forward to it.

They found a seat in the back of the food court, near one of the big windows that looked out over the river. The light seemed different at this level. Not any less leaden certainly but somehow more dramatic. Sitting across from her, watching her stir in extra sugar, both of them framed in the window, backlit by the sky. It felt like a movie or an Edward Hopper painting. Something from an earlier time, when being small and insignificant didn't matter, when it was something to be proud of. The good old days when noir lurked at the edge of our culture and had not yet taken its place at the center of life. When only film makers and artists had dark visions.

He thought of Tess's father, a regular working stiff who had sent his daughter to college and died believing it was this misstep—this hubris—and not the effects of two world wars and endless third world conflicts that had destroyed the century's values, its love of progress and belief in a good future.

Grandpa had died of lung cancer, even though he never smoked. He worked in a tile factory loading bags of asbestos. He had made his wife promise not to call the lawyer back, to stay away from OSHA. Christian was little but he remembered. "The men will lose their jobs," he said. And that had been enough to end the argument. What would his grandfather think now? Would he be proud of Christian who worked so hard and never had any time for himself. Or would he believe that Doomsday was just another assembly line, one that you needed a college degree to be hired on?

"You're smiling," she said, dimpling herself as though it were contagious. "It's nice to see you smile. You always look so serious. You know everyone but you never talk. And no one calls you Chris. Always Christian. Even Slater."

"I was wondering if we'd do it differently," he said, his eyes on an ore boat crawling past the window. "You know, if we had to do over. If it was our turn—"

"You mean the code?"

"I mean everything—the whole century! All the wars and the Holocaust and now the plague—cancer and AIDS, the final proof that we're living at a toxic pace on a planet that can no longer sustain life—!" Christian stopped. The ore boat was still framed in the window and already he had made a fool of himself.

Julie—was that her name?—was still stirring her coffee. Finally, she looked up. "Maybe you should have had a latte," she said quietly.

Christian laughed in spite of himself.

"Really." She was chewing on the little wooden stick. "You look like my son when he's ready for his nap."

"I'd like to meet your son." Christian surprised himself. "Some Sunday maybe, the three of us, at the

Zoo . . . or someplace." Her gaze was steady and direct. Christian rattled on, like a car without brakes careening down a hill. "I used to be a son once myself." Maybe a truck.

"He usually spends the weekends with his father. But we could do something. On Saturday if you like."

Tess was not pleased, even though he had waited all night for just the right moment to tell her. After dinner. As they lingered over coffee. "Saturday?! But that's our subscription night. You remember? Shostakovich? The Leningrad Symphony?"

Of course he hadn't. "You can get someone else. One of your girlfriends. Lena—she'd love to go!"

"Lena can't afford the Symphony. That's why I asked you in the first place."

"She can have my ticket—for free. It'll be a little present. I like Lena. What's the matter now?"

"Nothing."

"Can't I give away my ticket if I want? You know I don't care about the music. Last time I fell asleep and embarrassed you."

"I certainly can't force you to go if you don't enjoy it."

"Tess!" he crowed. "You're jealous!"

"I certainly am not—"

"Finally, after all these years! Me crying dramatically against the sofa cushions and you sweeping out on the arm of some Lothario who would probably show up for breakfast!"

"That is not true! I was very careful. The only man

I ever let into my bed was Tommy. And that was only because you seemed to like him."

"Stop babbling. Can't you tell when I'm teasing
you?" He grabbed her wrist, seeing as if for the first time,
the fine network of wrinkles around her eyes

"How did you get so grown up all of a sudden?"

"Did I mention she's just like you? She even has a
son."

"A son!" Tess's eyes narrowed suspiciously. "How
old?"

"Forty-six."

"That's disgusting?!"

"I meant the son. I was thinking that maybe we
could double. Don't hit me! I mean it now! That really
hurts!"

"You're lucky I don't kill you." Tess stopped snapping her napkin at him. "You really like her, don't you?"

"I don't know. I've only just—yes. Yes, I do."

"Be careful. Especially of the son."

"Was I so bad?"

"You were an angel"

It seemed to him that she hugged him extra hard
when he left that night. Before she could break out the
brandy. Before it got too late. Because the moon was full
and he wanted time to himself.

It was the last time he saw her alive.

She called him on Thursday night during the Bulls
game. Christian sighed and muted the sound.

"Did I pick a bad time?"

"No, no, it's fine. Jesus!" he muttered in spite of himself as the play passed to the other side of the court.

"I had an idea for a story, something I'll need your help with—is that you muttering? What's the matter?"

"Nothing, go ahead." The clock had come up on the screen. He sat forward frowning just as Tess stopped talking. The silence at the other end sounded expectant. "I'm sorry. I couldn't quite—"

"You haven't heard a word I've said!"

"Yes, I—"

"Tell me then. Tell me what I said."

"Something about a story—"

"It has to do with your work. It's a kind of dooms-day thing."

"Doomsday—you mean Slater and the group?"

"No, I mean doomsday in the generic sense, you know, the Millennium."

"Yeah . . ?"

"You sound doubtful."

"It sounds corny, you know, overdone. Besides, isn't it a little late to be writing a story about the Millennium? It's just around the corner. You won't have time to get it published."

"That's why I need your help. Stop groaning."

"I'm not groaning." The Lakers had the ball and the play skidded to the other side of the court.

"Here's my idea. What would happen if the computers didn't get fixed in time? If all over the world at midnight, the computers read the date as 1900 and . . ."

"Yeah?

"We were all catapulted back in time to the beginning of the 20th century."

"Jesus, Tess!"

"I have this image of a huge digital clock, just at the moment when the numbers change. A little whirring noise, then the metal flags fall into place. But it's not 2000, it's 1900 all over the world and the force of that moment is strong enough to—"

"What metal flags—"

"Those little metal flags that make the numbers."

"You're thinking of that old clock radio you had when I was a kid. They don't make those anymore. It's like an old scoreboard. Nowadays everything is digital. You can get a digital clock for $5 at Kmart."

"All right, then it's digital. That's even more dramatic . . . Red on black . . . the readout in Times Square . . . January 1, 1900 . . . !"

"Is it okay if I call you back?"

"But I need your help, you know . . . with the technology."

"Tess—" Be patient, he told himself. For 28 years she's had you all to herself. "What does your agent say?"

"She thinks it's a good idea. But I'll have to work fast."

"There's the turn of the century exhibit at the museum."

"Do you want to go? On Sunday," she added quickly. "I can make us a nice dinner and you can tell me all about—"

He wondered if she would say it, if she would admit what this was really about. Come on, Tess, he rooted for her to tell the truth, just this once. Stop living in a fantasy world.

". . . About the kind of computer glitch that would send us all back in time. I was thinking of a giant force field that jiggles all the molecules . . . or something. The way water boils in a pan. The bubbles move faster and faster and finally they erupt in steam!"

"The Caldron of Time?"

"That's it! I knew you'd have a good idea."

"Okay, mom. I'll call you on Sunday." By the time he hung up he was laughing.

"My mother has a theory—" he told her as they sat sipping brandy, their knees touching under the little table.

"Your mother—?"

"About us—about our jobs, I mean," he amended hastily.

"What an odd time to mention your mother."

Her lips were full and red. He had been watching them shamelessly for the last half hour. And her skin was very white. So white that the little blue veins made a shadow near her temples and just above the neck of her dress. He was afraid to follow the line below to the place where the fabric clung to her breasts. So he watched her mouth instead all night long while she talked of nothing really, work and her son and her life. The marriage that hadn't worked because they were too young and the child that made it all worthwhile.

"My parents were divorced before I was born," he told her. "My father took off for California and my mother raised me alone—" He was suddenly aware of the pressure of her knees under the table. "It's late," he mumbled, suddenly afraid of the images tumbling in his mind, images that he could see reflected in her eyes and feel in the pressure of her knee.

"Should we go?" he asked her.

She nodded. "Back to my place, there's no one there."

He should go out more, he reflected briefly gasping for air, like a man going down for the third time, his life passing before his eyes. Stop, he told himself, stop, this is important. You've got to do it right. But it didn't matter. There was some grace in the moment that swept them both away, that made it right no matter how awkward and breathless he felt. She felt it, too, pressing up against him as hard as she could, the same hunger.

And so it happened. And he was like a man dreaming or drowning until he awoke at last, drenched in sweat, exhausted and happier than he could ever remember. She was still beside him, stroking him, petting him. The sweat was drying on his body and he could feel faintly the first slight chill when she rolled on top of him, her hair tickling his chest. "You never told me," she said, "about your mother and her theory."

Tess had said that she would meet him at the museum at 2:30. He called earlier than he planned—on Saturday afternoon in a panic about what to wear. She offered to iron his collarless shirt, the one with the Tortoise shell buttons that she'd gotten him for Christmas. "I'm just about to grill some cheese sandwiches—the way you like them with Dijon mustard and a slice of plum tomato." As if he cared about Dijon mustard at a time like this. He listened as long as he could to the purr of triumph in her voice. She was so happy to have him back, her little boy, who was so picky about his food.

"Thanks, but I think I just figured it out. I'll wear my black sweater and the tweed sport jacket. I like those clothes. I feel good in them. I—I'm sorry to bother you with something so silly. I just panicked but I'm okay now. I've got to go."

"Black sweater? You mean the banlon with the long sleeves or the—"

"I'll figure it out. See you tomorrow." She was still talking when he put down the receiver. 2:45. Christian shrugged off a slight tremor of guilt. She'd have to get used to him living his own life. It was time, past time. The Twentieth Century. Christian stepped forward to study the display while he waited.

Fin de Siecle, that's what they called it, the End of an Era. How romantic it sounded, how unlike the abrupt and cryptic Y2K. Life was now in code and time stretched endlessly forward, the Millennium only a blip, as they hurried along—to what?— he wondered idly, then decided it didn't matter. Whether you faced the future purposefully like J.P. Morgan in the poster size picture hanging next to the display or the Italian immigrant radiant with hope beside him or the helmeted GI fatigued beyond endurance or the famous sailor kissing the girl at the end of the war. All these images were only that, images. Time happened. It carried you forward, ready or not.

Only 1127:30:17 hours left to the years 2000. Christian watched the electronic dots dance as the display changed. Change happened, moment to moment, faster than the brain could assimilate. Time was when hours accumulated slowly, sweeping past in a slow and stately march like the hands of an old clock. Eras gave way to epochs. But digital time was fragmented and meaningless, reduced to a level that the mind could not follow. Who was the Greek who posited that movement was not possible because each step could be bisected and then bisected again until the notion of progress became so minute as to be meaningless.

Like the old phrase that had always puzzled him. The reach exceeded the grasp. What did that mean exactly? That in the desire to see and be and encompass everything one lost it all, it fragmented and fell through your hands reduced to powder and sub atomic particles that could no longer be seen. What is the measure of a man, Christian wondered, his hands jammed into his pockets as he wandered through the dimly lit displays. On what scale should he aspire to live when all and nothing were in the final analysis the same.

Christian turned sharply his heart racing. Through the glass case out of the corner of his eye while he examined the Foucault pendulum he had caught sight of a face. White skin and platinum hair and a mouth as red and full as a peony. Was it Julie? Had she followed him here? Christian shivered with excitement but when he looked up she was gone if she had ever been there at all. He could still smell her on his skin and the thought of her made every hair on his body stand on end. Now he was seeing things.

Definitely not a day to be spent in a museum.

Damn it, where was Tess? Christian started. The man standing at the far end of the Century of Progress room with his hands clasped behind his back, surely that was . . ."Mr. Gartner?" Christian cleared his throat and tried again. "Mr. Gartner, sir?"

The figure whirled to face him. There was a moment of irritation, hostility almost until the older man composed his face and extended his hand. "Ah, young . . . Wahrmutter, Christian isn't it? Enjoying the exhibit?"

"Yes, sir. Very much, sir. And you?"

"Come here every chance I get. Wonderful man," he nodded toward the Wizard of Menlo Park, pictured in his laboratory, sleeves rolled up, hard at work inventing the twentieth century.

Christian remembered that he had seen the name of Hieronymous Gartner and that of the Doomsday Group on the list of the exhibit's sponsors. "They say he was eccentric," he blurted without thinking.

"What's that?"

"Edison. Didn't he fix up his birthplace like a museum and entertain guests dressed in period costumes . . . ?

"That was Ford, I'm afraid. He created a museum at Deerfield that included his birthplace as well as Edison's laboratory."

Christian flushed, realizing that he had just lost whatever chance he had to make a good impression. "I knew Edison was in there somewhere," he mumbled, then slowly his confidence returned. "I've always been fascinated by the inventor geniuses of that era. There's no room for that kind of individualism in the world today."

"Thank god for that!" The older man smiled, his

face dissolved in an expression of such charm that Christian was momentarily dazzled. They said that Mr. Gartner had arrived in the city with little except dreams in his pocket and that he had charmed his investors into founding the Doomsday Group. At a moment like this Christian could believe all the rumors. "How are we treating our own young geniuses?"

"Pardon . . ?" Christian smiled foolishly.

"Don't be coy, Wahrmutter. Are we paying you enough?"

"No, sir. I meant yes. . ."

"Which is it?" The blue eyes bore into him like lasers. "Mr. Slater tells me that you're the best we have. You can work circles around the others. Is that true?"

"Yes, but—"

"Never be afraid to be the best, Wahrmutter." Mr. Gartner draped an arm around his shoulder and steered him away from the Century Of Progress. "I'm glad that you're satisfied but if the day ever comes when you're not, I want you to see me first. I don't want you going over to the competition for something as ephemeral as money."

"No, sir, I won't."

Mr. Gartner reached inside his breast pocket for a silver card case and matching pen. While Christian stared, he extracted a card and scrawled a number hastily on the back. "My private line," he explained. Christian hesitated a moment before taking it from his outstretched hand.

"Now enjoy the rest of the exhibit." Mr. Gartner left him at the door to the Century of Progress Room and disappeared into the crowd. Christian felt an immense relief, a wave of exhaustion, as though he had battled some great force and somehow won his freedom. Tess would want to hear about this. He looked at his watch and frowned. 4:00. She often kept him waiting but this was too much. Another hour and the museum would be closed.

He was heading for the hall in the hope of finding a telephone when a placard on an easel near the door caught his eye. "New Year's Eve Gala," it read, in old fashioned turn-of-the-century letters. Christian smiled. This year he would not be alone. The poster showed President McKinley and his wife Ida arriving for a ball on December 31, 1899. "See in the Millennium with the great and near great of the last century," it read. "Join us for a costume party at Glessner House in the Prairie Avenue Historic District. Attend the Party of the Century hosted by Hieronymous Gartner and the Doomsday Group."

It was dusk by the time he rounded the corner onto his mother's street. He had called several times from the museum. Each time he got the machine. "This is Tess Wahrmutter. I'm sorry I can't come to the phone . . . "

"Tess? Tess, are you there? Pick up! Pick up for god's sake. Mom? It's me, Chris!" he had finally shouted into the receiver, realizing that something must be wrong, that Tess for all her scatterbrained preoccupation wouldn't have forgotten entirely a date she had made only the day before.

By the time he reached the house he was frantic. He know something was wrong as soon as he opened the door. The kitchen reeked of scotch. He fumbled for the light then stared at the broken tumbler at his feet, the pool of liquid long dry. "Tess!" He called, "Tess!"

He found her near the foot of the stairs, the angle of

her head bearing eloquent witness to the nature of her fall. She was wearing her company robe and the silly gold shoes. She must have lost her footing on the stairs and pitched headlong. The broken decanter lay shattered on the tiles, the glass still intact had rolled under a chair. "Tess," he crooned, stroking her hair, knowing already that she could not hear. "Mom!" It must have happened hours ago, last night while he was . . . "Mom, I'm sorry," he cried softly. Her robe had come undone and one large white breast lolled out carelessly. Otherwise she seemed composed and at peace. Her face had been carefully made up and she was wearing a shade of lipstick he had never seen. The smell of scotch was everywhere.

Hieronymous Gartner studied his reflection in the glass. His face superimposed on that of Edison. The great inventor caught in the sepia tones of a lost era, his own face looming larger than life beside him and more real. A soft insistent ring, he reached for the wafer thin telephone in his breast pocket. The voice in his ear sounded as though the man himself were standing next to him. A few short words and the connection was broken. Hieronymous Gartner smiled. The wizard of Menlo Park could rest easy. Giants still roamed the earth.

TWO

"**W**ould you say that your mother had a drinking problem?"

"I certainly would not!" Christian could hear the trembling in his voice. He gripped the arms of his chair.

"Didn't drink at all then?"

"I wouldn't say that," Christian tried to sound reasonable. He felt disoriented, isolated from his own body like a heavy equipment operator, sitting high up in his little cab, pulling levers and praying he could control what happened next. He sensed that his actions were very big, his voice too loud but that he himself was small and very far away.

The policeman looked at him expectantly. He was young and sandy-haired, someone that Christian might have gone to school with or met after work at the health club.

"A social drinker," Christian struggled to remember the term. "I would say she was a social drinker."

"Drank on weekends, then?"

"Yes, on weekends, certainly, and sometimes with dinner, you know, a little wine."

"What about late at night, if she couldn't sleep or before she went to bed? You say she lived alone?" Christian nodded. "Did she ever have a little nightcap?"

"Not scotch!" Christian could hear his voice rising. "I keep telling you, she didn't drink scotch. She only kept it in the house for—for—"

"Visitors?"

"I guess."

"Was she expecting anyone that evening? A date maybe?"

"My mother didn't go on dates, not any more, but she had a lot of friends."

"What kind of friends?"

"What do you mean?"

"Men? Women?"

"All kinds of friends, she was a very friendly person."

"But she wasn't entertaining anyone that evening?"

"Not that I know of."

"And you last saw your Mother?"

"On Tuesday night. But we talked on Thursday— she called me during the Bulls game—and again on Saturday afternoon."

"But she didn't tell you about her plans?"

Christian shook his head. "We talked about what I

was doing that night. She made some suggestions about—about—" he tried to talk around the lump rising in his throat—"about what I should wear and . . . she wanted me to come for lunch but I couldn't," Christian could feel his voice breaking, "I just couldn't."

"That's all right," The officer patted his back awkwardly. "We all have mothers. God forbid we should—well. Did you know she was on anti-depressants?"

"No, she would have said something."

"We found a bottle of Prozac in the medicine chest."

"I spent a lot of time with my mother. My tooth brush was in the medicine chest. I would have noticed."

"Doctor's name is R.L. Saunders. Ring a bell?"

"No, absolutely not, wait—"

"We found his name in her calendar, too. She had a standing appointment, 4:00 on Wednesdays, for the past 6 months."

"That's not possible. My mother and I were very close. I would have known."

"If your mother was feeling bad, she might have wanted to spare you. You know how mothers are—"

"My mother was not a drunk and she didn't need a shrink," he held up his hand to stem the flow of banalities he could see forming behind the policeman's eyes. "Let me finish! She didn't entertain men in her robe on Saturday night or drink Scotch on an empty stomach or—"

"Whoa, whoa. Listen to me. I know you're upset. But none of those things are wrong or even unusual for a lady your mother's age living on her own. People get older, they get lonely and they don't necessarily tell their kids— "

"My mother was not alone," Christian insisted, shouting to be heard over the sobs rising in his throat. "She had me!"

The police looked around, just long enough to be polite, then sent the body directly to the funeral home. There would be no autopsy, no coroner's investigation, no yellow crime scene tape encircling the house. Christian had been unable to convince even the young policeman in whom he had sensed some sympathy that the circumstances surrounding his mother's death were suspicious or anything more than they appeared to be. The officer had convinced him instead, talked him out of spending the night in his mother's house, to communicate with her one last time, to collect evidence, simply to be there in case some mysterious scotch drinking stranger showed up. "It's not good for you," the policeman had insisted and dropped him at his own apartment.

He punched in the number Julie had given him and pictured the telephone ringing in the empty bedroom. He tried her again and again, every time he thought of it. No answer, not even a machine. Finally he fell asleep with the television on. The next morning he drove to the funeral home. It was on the south side, near the house where Tess had grown up, the church she had gone to with her mother and father, before education and experience had made her an atheist.

"You're not really an atheist," he had insisted in the squeaky know-it-all voice of adolescence, "more like an agnostic."

"Don't tell me what I am!" She had snapped on the radio. They were driving somewhere, *she* was driving.

"Do you deny the existence of god," he persisted, "or do you simply question his relevance to the human condition? You have to think about God to be an atheist."

"Think about what? Nothing?" She turned the volume up. "You don't know what you're talking about. But like every man I've ever known, you insist on explaining everything. All you do is expose your ignorance."

Who had she been talking to really? Ten years later he could wonder. At the time he had believed himself her equal and her true adversary, the center of her world as she still was of his. "I'm an anarchist," he said, interrupting a silence that had lasted for many miles.

Tess had laughed so hard she had to pull the car over.

He had the address of the funeral home on the seat beside him, but the building was so discreet that he drove around the block several times before realizing that the large white old fashioned house was not a house at all but Thatcher Randall and Sons. "They're good people," the young policeman had assured him. "They'll take care of you." As he parked in the rear, he realized that he should have been suspicious of a house like this in what was otherwise a commercial district. Then again, Thatcher Randall specialized in disguising death, making it seem "nice" and "homey." It wasn't until he was mounting the steps that he took his inability to recognize the building for what it was: simple avoidance.

He was met at the front door by Thatcher Randall

himself or maybe it was only a son with the same name or maybe this was a franchise like Kentucky Fried Chicken, presided over by a mythical Southern Colonel no longer associated with the business. Maybe there was no Thatcher Randall or maybe they were all Thatcher Randall, each director assuming the name in turn to reassure the bereaved. The Mr. Randall who shook his hand and led him down a thickly carpeted hallway was old enough to have grown sons, still young enough to be the second generation. Just about his mother's age or maybe a little younger, with receding hair and kind eyes and a very expensive suit. Christian sat up and tried to pay closer attention. He had heard stories of people, not exactly cheated, but persuaded into funerals they couldn't afford.

Tess would come back from the dead if he spent a lot of money on anything as middle class as a funeral. In fact, now that he looked around he doubted that she would like this place at all. It was too much like a movie or the set of one of those old sitcoms, *Father Knows Best*. Hadn't he heard that Robert Young was gay? Maybe Tess herself had told him. Focus, Christian, he told himself. Focus. "It's not too late to have her cremated, is it? I'm sorry," he amended when he saw the startled look on Mr. Randall's face, "This all seems very unreal."

"Did your mother want to be cremated? Did she leave any instructions?"

"She didn't leave anything," Christian spread his hands out in front of him. "No will, no burial policy, no estate. She hadn't expected to die so soon," he heard himself explaining and deep inside the unspoken echo, she hadn't really expected to die at all. "I have a job," he added, in case the older man thought he was trying to shrug off his responsibilities, "and some savings. It's just that I can't do anything too . . . extravagant."

"We'll guide you to something simple and tasteful."

"Tasteful," Christian repeated after him, liking the word. "My mother had very good taste but she didn't like anything showy or sentimental or . . . " Christian hesitated, wondering how far he could go without giving offense.

Mr. Randall was sitting forward with his head slightly cocked as though he was looking forward to anything Christian might say and somehow that he couldn't be shocked . . . that Christian could say anything. Yes? the raised eyebrows seemed to urge, it's all right, tell me.

"Middle class," Christian licked his lips. "She was a free spirit, a writer," he added, eager to clarify her image and to give it an aura of respectability.

"I understand," Mr. Thatcher bobbed his head discreetly. "Something simple, but not plain. Something unique. Is there a female relative, someone who could help. . . " He let the sentence trail off.

Julie's image rose up before him, eyes closed, lips slightly parted, the upper lip fleshy and slightly beaded with sweat . . ."I called her agent this morning but she won't be here until tomorrow."

"Then we'll take care of it."

"Thank you," Christian stood up. The discreetly patterned walls were closing in on him. It was something in the air, the scent of flowers or maybe it was air freshener.

"I'm afraid we're not finished yet," Mr. Randall followed him to the door. "I'll need some information . . ."

Christian nodded. He could feel the sweat breaking out on his forehead. The year of his mother's birth? He thought it was 1950. Her college? Sorry, someplace in the Midwest, he thought. There was a yearbook somewhere. His mother's agent would know. It was probably on her book jacket. Any other newspapers that should carry the death notice? Why? There may be relatives or friends, Mr. Randall hedged, what about—what about your father?

"What about him?" Christian felt his fists clench as his weight settled back in his heels.

"Does he need to be notified? I can do that for you, if you'd like."

"I don't know."

"You can think about it, of course, but not too long . . ."

"I don't know who my father is."

"Well, in that case . . . Come into my office, why don't you, son. Sit down. We don't need to do all this in the hall."

"It's all right."

"Come in and sit down. We'll have some coffee."

Christian took a deep breath and allowed himself to be led back into the office. Sitting in the chair on the other side of the desk, watching Mr. Randall pour the coffee, add two lumps of sugar and search for the creamer, Christian had a feeling of familiarity, as though he had awakened from a bad dream to find himself in the midst of a comforting ritual. Or maybe this was the dream.

"My mother loved old movies," he said, reaching for the coffee. The funeral director served them both from china cups and saucers. Tess would have liked that. It's the little things that matter, she always said. "She used to read ahead in the guide and program the VCR to tape at any hour of the day or night. She was always taping something and she never threw anything away. We had shelves of movies . . . hundreds . . . thousands. . . ."

The man nodded.

"Andy Hardy was my favorite. Isn't that corny?"

Mr. Randall stirred his coffee.

"I always wanted to sit down some night with the judge and talk through my life, hear him tell me not to worry. She used to tell me that all the time, but I didn't believe her. I wanted to hear it from a man, someone who was more like me . . . my father."

Christian realized that his face was wet. "She wouldn't tell me who he was. Never. My grandfather claimed that she didn't know. They used to fight about it sometimes, when we went to visit at the holidays. Late at night, when I was supposed to be asleep."

"What did you think of all that?"

"I used to pinch myself to stay awake so I could listen. Maybe she'd drop some clue or say his name out loud. But I always fell asleep. It was like waiting for Santa Claus. The next morning I could never tell how much was real and how much was a dream. Finally I decided to take matters into my own hands. I went through her old photo albums and I found a man who seemed to speak to me. I couldn't see his face too clearly and that seemed right somehow. He had his shirt off and he was squinting into the sun. Even in the picture I could tell that he was lonely. I thought that was important. Because I was lonely, too. It would have been easy to pick one of the handsome boys, whose faces showed up again and again in her album. But there was only one picture of "him," the one I called my father. And that seemed right, too. As though she had tried but couldn't quite bring herself to destroy all the evidence."

"Did you keep the picture?" Mr. Randall prompted.

"Oh, no. I couldn't do that." Christian was genuinely shocked. "I was a spy, you see, and I couldn't afford to do anything that would bring attention to myself. But I went back to the book every chance I got until—" Christian held out his cup for a refill. "One day I forgot and after that it didn't seem so important."

"Don't blame her, son. She must have had her own reasons."

"Maybe my grandfather was right. Maybe she just didn't know." Christian looked around. "There must be something for me to sign."

Mr. Randall shook his head.

"I think I explained that my mother had no insurance. I can make some kind of deposit today." Christian reached for his checkbook.

"That won't be necessary."

"I don't understand."

"Someone called earlier from the Doomsday Group. A Mr. Slater, I believe. It's all been taken care of."

THREE

T he day of the viewing was the longest day of his life. Her agent came and sat beside him on the hard wooden chairs. The Doomsday Group sent flowers and a few of the programmers showed up led of course by Slater, tastefully dressed in a black silk suit with a collarless shirt of the same color.

"You look like a funeral director," Christian told him, shaking his hand. "Actually, you look better than the funeral director."

"Sorry for your loss," he said pumping Christian's hand.

"Listen," Christian held onto his hand. Slater looked startled. "Mr. Randall told me what you did. I don't know how to thank you but I just wanted to let you know that I'm good for it. I'll sign a note or whatever as soon as I'm back at work."

"No need," Slater finally succeeded in pulling his hand back. "Company policy."

"It's company policy to pay for family funerals?"

Slater nodded. "Take your time getting back to work," he said, "take as long as you need." Then he retreated to a seat in the back row where he sat without speaking for a half hour or more, then rose abruptly as if obeying some inner timepiece, signed the guest book and left.

"Strange guy," Christian muttered to no one in particular. His mother's agent had gone outside for a cigarette. Christian sat alone in front of the coffin, staring into space, willing Julie to appear in the doorway, holding her son's hand, leading him with small careful steps.

"What's his name?" he had asked, only three nights ago, but already it seemed like a lifetime.

"Ethan," she had whispered, her hair brushing his cheek, the spice of her perfume lingering, taking on a life of its own in the air beside him. "Nathan?" he repeated, because the bar was so noisy. So she told him again, coming even closer the second time, resting her hand on his sleeve in a gesture of easy familiarity. It was the first time they had touched.

He had been over the details of their brief night together so many times they had worn a track in his memory. That slight hesitation when they finally faced each other in the elevator, how he leaned down, her face growing larger until he closed his eyes and let it overwhelm him, the way his palm fit in the hollow of her back, the streetlight outside her bedroom window. Recalling any one of a hundred details, a thousand, was like pushing the play button. One thought was all that it took to start the feature running again.

He sat in a daze in front of his mother's coffin, waking periodically when someone like Slater showed up to pay his respects, or the young policeman dressed in a suit and smelling of aftershave, locking eyes, then shifting his gaze too quickly as though he were ashamed of the intensity of his own grip or the kind impulse that had brought him to pay his respects. Perhaps it was more than that.

McAuliffe—was that his name?—he had seen it on his badge and again in the book after he left, Bernard McAuliffe. The man was probably fingering him for the crime, following him to his mother's grave, watching for some telltale signs. Or maybe it was just that he was Irish. You know how they are, Tess's voice whispered in his ear, terrified of their own feelings. What kind of feelings would they be, Christian wondered idly, to send his eyes skittering away like that, like an animal frightened by the sound of human feet.

Helen was coming back, threading her way toward him through the rows of empty chairs. Helen Carver, his mother's agent. Such a purposeful name, Christian thought it was probably made up. Everything else about her was nondescript from the faded blond hair to the pale face marked with the faint scars of acne and the two piece separates she favored. Dark skirts topped with sporty blazers, checks and plaids in coordinating colors. Dressy but not too dressy. Business-like but not too business-like.

She wore very little makeup—a little gloss on her lips, pale neutral polish on her square-cut nails. Christian couldn't look at her without wondering if she were a dyke, if perhaps she nursed a secret passion for his mother. That was the reason she had dropped everything and caught the first plane from LaGuardia to O'Hare. Or maybe it wasn't even secret. Maybe—

"There are more things in heaven and earth, Horatio," he could hear the scorn in Tess's voice, "than are dreamt of in your philosophy." If ever he dared to ask the question, her indignation would have driven him back. He would have turned it into a joke. "My name's not Horatio!" waggling his fingers and wiggling his eyebrows in that Groucho way that always made her laugh. God, he missed her. Already, he missed her so much.

Hot tears were welling up and he just had time to brush them away as Helen reached his chair, the faint smell of cigarettes clinging to her clothes.

"You want a tick-tack?" She shook a clump of the little green pills on her palm and held it out to him.

"Sure. Thanks. Grieving is pretty hard on your breath."

"We could get something to eat."

"There's a deli tray in the kitchen," he told her, "and the neighbors brought desserts. If you're hungry—"

"I was thinking about you, actually."

"I'm okay." He glanced down at the purse she had settled on the floor between them, a kind of bucket, like a horse's feedbag, with two soft folds of buttery leather at the top. "Is that a Coach bag?"

"Yes, it is," she sounded surprised.

"Thought so," he nodded wisely as his eyes wandered to the flowers and to his mother's profile just visible over the top of the casket. It was the last time he would see her. In just a few day's time he would long for even this much sight of her. But he couldn't seem to appreciate it, couldn't seem to stay with the experience the way he wanted to, the way he thought he should. One day he would reproach himself, he knew. One day he would long for this day to come again.

"How do they know what color makeup to use, you know, on her face?" He was staring at his mother's nose, the tip of it that rose above the casket. It didn't really look like Tess. That was the problem. Something about the lips painted in that pale pink shade, that was supposed to look natural but ended up grayish instead because no blood flowed underneath. And the width of the nostrils through which the breath no longer flowed, and the nose itself so definite and so still as though it were carved out of stone.

"Didn't they ask you for her makeup and a picture?"

He shook his head.

"They're supposed to," she looked around vaguely as though she were in a restaurant and the waiter had disappeared.

"It's all right," he added, afraid that she might be about to complain. "She looks fine."

"I know you're not hungry," Helen continued after a pause. "But let's go out anyway. Just for a little while. There are some things I need to discuss with you. Do you mind?" She laid her hand lightly on his knee. A dyke would never do that. "Just for a while."

"No, I don't mind, if you think it's okay—" he indicated his mother with a nod of his head, "to leave her I mean."

"Just for a little while," she glanced at her watch. Christian reached for the leather straps before she could and handed the purse up to her. What surprised him the most was the obvious financial statement, he thought as he trailed her out of the parlor. He had a theory—he could remember mentioning it once to Tess—that Helen dressed nondescriptly so that her clients would forget about all the money she was making from them. The Coach bag was definitely a blip in the strategy. Or maybe she had grown careless, more willing to express herself, now that Tess was dead.

"Come on," she smiled kindly as he caught up with her. "We'll go to that little coffee shop across the street. We won't even move the car."

"Are you sure you won't have anything else? A sandwich maybe?" she asked him when they were seated in a corner booth and had placed their orders.

"Just the coffee is fine."

"You've been living on coffee—"

"Works for me!" he cut her off, then added—just so that he wouldn't seem rude or ungrateful, "I'll get a sandwich later, back across the street."

"There are some things you should know," she squared off her placemat, rearranging the silver so that each piece stood at the perfect angle, "about your mother's estate."

"I didn't know my mother had an estate," he laughed lightly willing her to look at him. It must be difficult in a business like hers to be so ill at ease with people.

She must prefer to work behind the scenes. To keep either a desk or a telephone between her and the world. The Formica table didn't provide the distance that she craved.

"Not in the ordinary sense of the word," she began earnestly. It was this earnest conscientiousness, he decided staring into the flat blue eyes ringed by pale unblinking lashes, this glimpse of the schoolgirl that gave her a certain charm. Her small breasts and unflinching sense of responsibility, even the aura of immaturity that clung to her. It wasn't Julie, his breath caught, as he recalled the vein pulsing in her neck, but there was a certain—

"Pay attention!" Tess's voice hissed in his ear, "This is important."

"As her son you have inherited," Helen smiled self-consciously, "not a large amount of money certainly, but some royalties and a certain number of copyrights that could become more valuable as time progresses. At the core of this estate is a network of relationships, arrangements, agreements, if you will, that must be managed . . ."

If you will? Who talked like that? Lawyers? Writers! That was it. She was a failed writer, probably a playwright, that's why she was so enamored of her work—He felt a faint kick under the table and drew back.

"I"m sorry," Helen blushed, "did I—?"

"That's all right," he said knowing it had been Tess. "What you're saying then—" he sat forward, willing her to make her point.

"Your mother made you her literary executor."

"Her literary—?"

"Executor," Helen prompted, folding her hands and settling back against the booth.

"But I can't—"

It means that you're responsible for her papers and the disposition of all outstanding contracts and copyrights. You decide what to publish and what to withhold."

"Why would I want to withhold anything?"

She slid a set of keys across the table.

"What's that?"

"Your mother's keys."

He pulled his hand back abruptly.

"This is everything," Helen fingered the key ring seductively. "Her files, her desk. I think there's a safe deposit key as well. Yes, here it is, the little one."

"This is a job for someone like you, someone who understands— I have my own work. I'm very busy."

"I'll advise you, of course, but the decisions are yours to make," she nudged the keys closer to him.

"I can't do this," he admitted flatly.

"This was her idea, Christian. The estate is small. She didn't want it eaten away with fees."

"But I don't know what to do!"

"Go to her office, read through her papers, make a list of what you find. Use her calendar to cancel appointments, check deadlines. She was very organized, you know," the lashes fluttered. "This was your mother's idea, Christian," she said, not sounding any happier than he was. His hands closed reluctantly on the keys.

"Besides," she continued quietly, "this will be good for you. Your mother knew that, too. It will help you come to terms."

"Tell me," he said after a moment, leaning toward her. "Were you—?" The eyes had changed color, like a pond under a cloudy sky, more grey now than blue. "Did you and Tess—?" She had grown up somewhere in the Midwest . . . Iowa? Ohio? She and Tess shared the same background. "Never mind," he said at last, "I guess I'll find everything I need to know in her papers."

They walked back together in silence, Helen holding him back at first from crossing the street, then taking his arm when she thought it was safe. They said goodbye at the door to the funeral home. "She had just begun work on a new project," Helen said after she had hugged him and he had felt the pressure of those hard little breasts against his chest.

"I know. She called me. Something about the Millennium."

"Better check her calendar. She may have made some appointments." She slung the Coach bag over her shoulder. Her heels made a loud, purposeful sound as she walked away.

He walked around for days with the keys jangling in his pocket, mixing with his spare change and subway tokens. Every night, he took them out and put them on top of his dresser. Every morning, he put them back in his pocket wondering if this would be the day.

Back at work Julie seemed distant and preoccupied. Her desk had been moved to the other side of the room, her place taken by a tall thin boy who wore headphones and swayed from side to side while he worked, sometimes humming a little louder than he realized or mouthing snatches of lyric and then just as abruptly falling silent. Christian thought about complaining, strode purposefully to the center of the room and waited, clinching and unclinching his fists while Slater fiddled with his papers.

How he longed to seize the top of the desk with both hands, to thrust himself into Slater's field of vision and hang there, looming over him, whistling tunelessly, staring vacantly into space. There, he would say, how do you like it? How long had he stood there before Slater looked up, pushed his glasses back up the bridge of his nose and smiled?

That afternoon Julie came back to her old desk. She motioned the tall thin boy away and sat for a few minutes in his place. She was wearing a short lavender dress that clung to her hips, her mouth smudged with purple, darker in the center, like the heart of a flower. "I heard about your mother," she said, reaching for his hand, "I—I'm sorry." She sat for a while pressing his fingers, willing him back to life. He said nothing, only watched as if from a great distance, while her thumb made circles in the heel of his hand. After a few minutes of silence, she stood and returned to her place on the far side of the room.

Her hair was so white that he spotted her easily, whenever he looked up, shining in her far corner like a star. A planet so distant it could never be seen in the present, every glimpse a look back into a past he no longer believed, a future he had only dreamed.

It was no surprise one day to find her gone, her desk cleared out, no word left behind as to her whereabouts. No surprise at all. He was a man accustomed to losses.

FOUR

Christian worked alone now every day in the simulation room. Seventeen computers had been networked together to form a complex closed environment that could be used to test their theories. "What would happen if . . . " Use your imagination, they told him, push the envelope.

"But what am I testing?"

"Whatever you want," Slater smiled like the Mona Lisa. "It's up to you. We don't want to be—taken by surprise."

Slater had materialized at his side without warning, while Christian was drumming his fingers on the desk. The boy in front of him, Julie's replacement—he had never bothered to learn his name—was swaying from side to side, under the spell of some CD. Reggae maybe from the sinuous insistence of his shoulders, the snap of his fingers and the occasional "Mon" that drifted into Christian's consciousness. "Take a break," Slater said, lifting one of the headphones and speaking directly into his ear. The boy scurried away and Slater slid into his seat.

Christian was dumbfounded. Never in the history of his employment had he seen Slater step down from his platform and into the ranks. He seemed out of place, like a grownup sitting in a child's desk at open house. "Not too bad, I hope?" Slater nodded in the direction of the retreating boy.

"No, no," Christian swallowed hard. He thought about the day he had meant to complain, the day after his mother's funeral. How long had he stood blankly in front of Slater until the man finally looked up and smiled? Had he really put his hands on either side of the desk and loomed over him, whistling tunelessly. He had been in such bad shape in the days after the funeral that he couldn't remember now if he had actually done it or only thought about it.

"You've been under a lot of strain," Slater shrugged. "You seem to be doing better now."

Christian flushed. He had pulled himself together through will power and strength of purpose. Slater's sympathy, his suggestion that Christian was somehow in need of special handling, infuriated him.

Slater was a big man with a prominent cleft in his chin. A halo of coppery curls shone around his head, making him look like the face on a Roman coin, a man of strength and purpose. But Christian knew better. He was just a big suit installed in the front of the room to keep order, a monitor, the officer stationed in front of the galley to beat time for the rowers. Now there was an idea. He saw Slater wielding his mallets. "Ramming speed," he called out in his slightly nasal voice as his glasses slid down the bridge of his nose.

Christian smiled and Slater nodded back cheerfully. "Hope you don't mind. We like to put the new ones near you, in case they need anything."

Christian nodded, remembering what Julie had told him. "I don't mind."

"As of today, it won't matter anyway."

Christian frowned. What was he up to now?

"You've been assigned to simulation. I just got the call."

"Simulation," Christian echoed, still wary.

Slater cleared his throat, time to change gears. He paused a moment and let a look of boyish sincerity settle on his features. "I don't need to tell you, we're running out of time. Operations like this are running full throttle all over the planet. We think we'll make it, we've pledged to make it. But in the mad dash for the finish, there may be something we've overlooked. That's where you come in—" Slater poised dramatically.

Christian willed the "Me?" rising in his throat to remain unspoken and concentrated on composing his features. He would not give Slater the satisfaction of taking him by surprise . . . he would not . . .

But the speech was over. Slater glanced down at his watch. "Mr. Gartner is waiting for us in the lab."

"The lab?" Christian couldn't stop himself.

"*Your* lab, I should say," Slater slid awkwardly out of his seat. "Come on, we can't keep the big man waiting."

Christian rose slowly. Around him everyone had fallen silent, pretending to be engrossed in their work. He was suddenly unwilling to leave the safety of the big room where they jostled against each other like a litter of puppies, competing for space, for privacy and information.

He longed for the noisy everyday sounds that would tell him everything was all right. "Are you still on the phone?" "Hey, do you still work here? Yeah, you! I need help." "Come here a second, come on, just for a minute. What are you doing that's so important?" Instead silence descended as he followed Slater down the row, their presence falling like a shadow on desk after desk.

Christian couldn't shake the feeling he was being punished. For a crime he didn't commit, couldn't even imagine. Nobody could. He was being locked away as a precaution, a preventive measure.

"I need to know you're safe," Tess had told him, "playing quietly in your room, where I can find you. Some mothers have to work outside their homes, you know. They send their children to stay all day with strangers." Christian nodded hopefully. He had seen those children racing through the playground, screaming with pleasure. "We're lucky because we can be together. I'm right next door in my office if you need anything."

They passed Julie's desk, still empty, Christian ran his hand along the surface, taking comfort from the smooth stability. How he longed to clutch at something, anything that might hold him back. But he was a fully grown man, too big to run under the table, holding onto the legs, sobbing with grief and rage as Tess pulled him away down the long hall to his room.

He had only done it once, forced her to handle him in that way, her hair flying in ragged wisps, her breath labored, her features swollen with rage. His brief rebellion had only made it worse, confirmed his helplessness. He learned to keep his rage inside, ignore the sounds of children outside his window. They didn't want him anyway. He couldn't play their games, first because he couldn't see well enough and later on because of his glasses.

He learned to play quietly as she had asked, the thick lenses reflecting first the light of a little black and white portable television and finally the neon glare of his first primitive Radio Shack. Oh happy day, when he unpacked the toy that was not a toy, his guide to the future, where he sat day after day inventing games that he could win until the sound of the other children receded and then disappeared and he emerged at last from the little room at the top of the stairs, a man that others envied, a man with a future.

A girl looked up and caught his eye, one of Julie's friends, he remembered their bright little dresses ringing her desk, their faces swaying like flowers over some problem in the code or maybe it was only a takeout menu. She smiled tentatively but it was enough. "What happens to all this . . . in January?" he heard himself ask, finally summoning the presence of mind to break the spell that hung between them as he trudged behind Slater like a condemned man.

"Oh, I don't know." Slater tried to sound amiable but evidently he found small talk as difficult as Christian himself. "They'll find something for us to do, I'm sure."

"But isn't there a plan?" he insisted, nearly frantic.

They were nearing the steel door with its dark rectangle of reflecting glass.

"No doubt there is. But *you* don't have to worry." Slater frowned peering into the smoke-colored window. He couldn't see in, but he peered anyway out of habit. "Mr. Gartner has enterprises all over the world. You'll be taken care of."

Evidently someone could see out and had been watching for them. Slater had just raised him hand to knock when a faint electronic hum and the click of the lock signaled that the door had been opened from the inside. They pushed inside quickly before the lock was reset.

"Here he is!" Hieronymous Gartner turned to greet them. "Well? How do you like your new domain?"

Christian swallowed. "Slater—" what was Slater's first name? Richard? And what did he go by? Dick? Rick? Rich? He couldn't call him Mr. Slater, not when he was being given his own lab. "He's just been telling me—"

"I'm sure *he* has." Gartner winked, their own private joke. "These are computers, Richard." Slater blushed. "He might not be a technical whiz, our Mr. Slater, but he's a dab hand at spotting those who are and getting them the resources they need. Isn't that right?"

Slater mumbled something and Gartner let him go, dropped him from the centrifuge of his vision so clearly that Christian could almost hear a thud.

"No doubt Richard has been telling you about these computers," Gartner winked again. "They've been networked to simulate a complex, closed environment. They *are* a complex closed environment," he corrected himself with a smile, "the simulation is up to you—"

"Actually he has, sir." Christian broke in, tired of all the winking and signaling.

Gartner paused in surprise. He was not used to interruptions or to any reaction that he had not actually cued himself. His staff were masters at reading these cues and it was for this skill and not for any other that he chose them.

"Mr. Slater—Richard—was explaining the network to me, but he couldn't really explain the nature of the tests, that is, the particular environment that you want me to simulate."

"Of course he couldn't. That's your job, if you want it—" Mr. Gartner paused again, but no answer was forthcoming.

Christian held himself ramrod stiff, like a soldier. It would take a crowbar to open his mouth. He would have this job on his own terms, he had decided, or not at all. He was the owner of his mother's house, after all. He could sit all day on the Internet, if he wanted, roaming chat rooms, playing computer games and letting his fingernails grow like Howard Hughes.

Gartner smiled, like the sun bursting through a bank of clouds. There would be no storm after all. Christian could feel himself relax, hear the sigh as Slater allowed himself to exhale. "*Our* job," Gartner's eyes twinkled with amusement, as though this were a joke that he had arranged or a test that Christian had passed with flying colors. "Our job—as you have rightly pointed out—" Gartner inclined his head ever so slightly in Christian's direction—"is to make you aware of our plans, our concerns, that will set the parameters of your simulation. Richard," he snapped, not his fingers exactly, but the effect was the same as Slater sprang for the panel set in the wall. He pressed a button and a map of the world descended soundlessly on the wall behind Gartner.

"Here in the United States we've been conditioned to think of a single moment of time as the starting point for the Millennium. Midnight, December 31, when the future becomes the present and the world enters the twenty-first century. But in point of fact, when the ball goes up in Times Square, the century will already be 17 hours old. The Millennium begins here," a point of light danced across the Pacific, as though Gartner were holding a laser wand, even though his hands were empty, "at the other end of the world, and it will move like a wave first through the newly restored Asian markets and then Europe, reaching London five hours ahead of New York. Since the world moves on Greenwich Mean Time, we might say that the Millennium actually begins here in Greenwich, then across the Atlantic to the United States from the eastern seaboard to the west coast and back out into the Pacific."

Slater was nowhere to be seen. He must have slipped behind some hidden panel and was even now pressing buttons and pulling levers to make a path of light for the new century. Ignore the man behind the curtain, Christian thought to himself, and in that moment Hieronymous Gartner seemed like a spiritualist, a charlatan, who made the table bump and knocks sound from the next room.

"But I can see you're not impressed," Christian jumped. He hadn't realized that Gartner was studying him so closely in the darkened room, hadn't thought he was studying him at all, had imagined him to be engrossed in his own pyrotechnics. "Lights, Richard!" Gartner barked. A little piece of dark paneling opened in the back of the room and Slater emerged, looking slightly dazed as the room flooded with light. "Our clients love this," Gartner shrugged deprecatingly. "We should have known better than to try it on the boy genius. You do get the point?"

"You're wondering what will happen in the 24 hours it takes the Millennium to cross the date line."

"Precisely," Gartner beamed. "What kind of chaos will it work in a wide area network, like our international banking system, for example, or our stock market, not to mention our satellite defense system when everything is out of synch?"

"Possibly nothing, sir," Christian couldn't stop himself. All those years in the room at the top of the stairs had conditioned him to be the bright boy, the one who answers first. "Given that these systems are always out of synch."

"Possibly," Gartner nodded, "even probably, but there's the rub. We won't *know* until it's too late to do anything, unless we act now. In fact now may already be too late." He glared at Slater, as though he had somehow dropped the ball and put the world at risk. Slater hung his head.

Is this an act? Christian couldn't help asking himself. Are these two for real? "You don't mean that multinational organizations haven't tested the implications of Y2K on their international networks?" Christian wondered aloud. "Especially in the light of Euro conversion, that would be suicide."

There it was again. The look. Gartner and Slater had exchanged another meaningful glance. Do we know how to pick them or what? "Richard?" Gartner deferred to his manager and stood with his hands in his pockets, gazing benignly from side to side.

Slater stepped forward on cue. "Mr. Gartner means that *we* haven't tested it, not as completely as we should, not just as a theory or a concept as Mr. Gartner did five years ago when he founded the Group, but *now*, now that most of the pieces are in place, and instead of speculating we can actually see what the software will do."

Gartner smiled with satisfaction. "We are the major firm engaged in this work around the globe. If the Wizard here were still behind the curtain—" Slater made a move but Gartner waved him back. "No, no, Richard, it's all right. Christian will just have to use his imagination. We could show you a map of the world with little red lights identifying all the operations of the Group."

"One thousand points of light—" Slater seconded.

"Not all direct employees, many of them, especially in the East are merely agents of the Doomsday Group. But the point is, we literally cover the earth and if we haven't tested it, you'll pardon the hubris, but it hasn't been tested."

Christian wished that he could see all the little red lights.

"Many of our clients are smaller businesses," Gartner continued, "without the vertical integration of a large multinational. These are the people who will literally be caught in the middle if some piece of the puzzle is missing. We owe it to them to at least predict where the problems are likely to occur so that they can plan now for damage control."

Christian nodded. Now it was beginning to make sense. It was like selling maintenance plans for your own appliances. Betting that something would go wrong with your own products, something outside the provisions of your warranty. The business wouldn't come to an end on January 1. It was only beginning.

"This room has been networked to represent a large hypothetical company with installations in seventeen different time zones," Gartner continued. "Your first job is to simulate the kinds of things that could go wrong all over the world and the effects on each part of the business. After you've mastered the implications within the relatively controlled environment of a closed system, you can move out in widening circles to explore the effects on companies outside the loop, the tiers of suppliers, customers, brokers, even contiguous industries. The possibilities are endless."

Christian blinked. He was right. "And the time is limited . . . ? " He let the sentence finish itself. If they hadn't bothered with simulation earlier in the game, what good would it do them now?

"Take some time to get used to the setup," Slater began, somewhat anxiously. "Write a few scenarios. Run some limited tests."

"Play with your toys," Gartner smiled.

"By myself?"

"You can requisition as many people as you need, from inside or outside the Group."

"With all due respect," Christian nodded to Mr. Gartner, "I don't see the point. If we've gotten along without this level of testing so far, what good will it do us now?"

"What good—?!" Slater sputtered with indignation.

"It's all right," Gartner raised his hand genially to ward off Slater's objections. "That's what we pay him for, you know, to see through our strategies, to tell us what's wrong before it happens. I appreciate your frankness, son." Gartner lingered ever so slightly on the word. "But surely you realize, that in a business like ours, no amount of technical window dressing ever goes to waste."

Slater nodded wisely. It was clear that he had no idea what Gartner was talking about.

"And that's my job, sir?" Christian countered. "To be in charge of window dressing?"

"Do you actually think that the Y2K problem will be over on January 1?" Gartner's eyes snapped with electricity. "The Pentagon won't finish its reprogramming efforts until the year 2010—that's a conservative estimate. Our business *begins* on January 1 when millions of people finally realize that the changes they've been putting off have already happened. When their business begins falling down around their ears, that's when we step in and really begin our work."

"All this," Gartner made a sweeping gesture that took in the men and women outside the steel door as well as the thousands of operatives around the globe, "all that's gone before is nothing but marketing, establishing us as a worldwide presence, *the* international authority on Y2K issues. When the year 2000 happens, we want to make sure that we're hooked up and ready to run. Because between you and me," Gartner lowered his voice confidentially, "No one knows what's going to happen. We can't possibly know. No matter how many tests we run."

Christian licked his lips. He should say something, but he didn't know where or how to begin.

"So what do you say? Are you with us?" Gartner was smiling now. "We won't sully the pure air of the lab with any talk of money—"

Slater giggled.

"Suffice it to say that when you walk outside this room, you'll be making twice what you were making when you walked in. That is, if you say yes."

Christian looked around the room, allowing himself for the first time to really take it all in. He shivered. It was cold. There was a white lab coat hanging on the back of the door. His.

"Yes," he said, smiling and shaking hands.

FIVE

uddenly he had a future again. He found himself working day and night, grabbing meals from the all night deli, coming home exhausted at all hours. He never watched the news anymore or bought a newspaper. He could write his name in the dust on his coffee table. In fact, he did. After staring for a moment he began making notes for a new test scenario on the back of a magazine. He dumped the contents of his hamper on the bathroom floor and began wearing the socks from the bottom of the pile a second time. He had never been happier.

Ideas came pouring out. Should he use one powerful computer to model the complexity of the world environment or should he do what Gartner had done, simply network or duplicate the actual number of places where something could go wrong. The closed network was faster, more efficient but it had an academic feel that he didn't like. Why simulate the real world when the Dooms-day Group had the resources to actually work in it?

Wouldn't the Group's worldwide facilities make better test sites? The random selection of equipment, the variance in facilities and resources, including the skill level of the testers would multiply the farther removed they were from the controlled environment of the lab. Even chance, the wild card, the possibility that something completely unforeseen and unrelated to the variables being tested could occur—a power surge or an outage of some kind—any type of external event that could not be controlled and might act as a drain on their resources, would have more scope, more reality, outside the lab.

Instead of centralizing the test function, putting all the testers in isolation in some high powered lab, the test function should be spread out. The best thing that Christian could do for the Group was to dismantle his new empire, to write a simple series of tests that could be distributed worldwide. If more brain power was needed, it would be not to conduct the test but to think through the results. Here again, it wasn't a "think-tank" ivory tower analysis that he had in mind. They would do better to form focus groups made up of many different kinds of intelligences—engineers, housewives, musicians, mechanics. The day of the pyramid was over. Top-down thinking would go out with the century. Christian's generation was the first to understand that the Earth was a small planet. Networking would maximize participation and make the results as well as the responsibility self-distributing.

Christian shuddered when he thought about the kind of staff he could assemble here at the Doomsday

Group. There were too many MBAs, people like Slater who had fallen into their work, stumbled into it from lack of a clear future as much as anything else or from some negative quality, a lack of imagination or a willingness to please. His best recruiting source would be university campuses. He should be pulling real thinkers from scientific programs, people who could work from inference like himself. What was this, after all, but another Manhattan Project? A race against time, a job of limited duration but great significance. What were they doing—any of them—that was more important than saving the world from chaos?

By the time he left the lab that night his heart was racing. The sky seemed deeper than he remembered, as though the kaleidoscope had shifted to reveal new dimensions spangled with stars. He couldn't face the dusty apartment with its musty closet smell. Was he wearing a clean shirt? He gave his shoulder a suspicious sniff. He needed a walk to air himself out, to flush the caffeine from his system. Almost without thinking, he found himself on Julie's street. Her lights were on. Was she entertaining? He saw a solitary figure cross and then recross the room.

On the next corner a telephone booth beckoned, an oasis of light. What if she were up so late because of her son? Maybe he was sick. Or maybe like him she was burning the midnight oil on a project. Where was she working now, he wondered. Why hadn't he made inquiries? He should have talked to Slater or to Human Resources. Why had he let her slip through his fingers?

He stood for a while longer watching the window, pondering his options, until the light went out. Then he glanced down at his watch and hurried home. Too tired to undress, he threw himself across the bed and fell into a deep dreamless sleep.

"I wouldn't advise it," Slater told him the next morning.

"Wouldn't advise what?"

"What you just said—"

"Going to human resources? Making inquiries?"

"Looking for trouble. The girl was no good," he added by way of explanation.

"What do you mean 'no good'?" He made a fist and began running it softly into his palm. He had a sudden urge to damage that classic profile, to make a new dent in the deeply cleft chin.

"She couldn't do the work. There was something wrong with her."

"Who hired her?"

"No one. I suppose I did. An agency sent her over."

"I thought we didn't work with agencies."

"We don't. That is I thought—just this once. These people had called before. We were so overloaded . . ."

"Did you clear it with anyone?" Silence. What a time to act on your own initiative. "So you don't really know who she is?"

Slater shook his head. "As soon as I realized—but by then she was gone."

"Have you discussed this with anyone? Does Mr. Gartner know?"

Slater blanched. Evidently not.

"What if she was sent here to learn our business? What if she compromised our security or my god, do you know the kind of liability an organization like this is under from viruses?"

"I was thinking that she might have been sent here for another reason."

Christian stared at the big man. The color was slowly returning to his face.

"She was pretty conspicuous for a spy. I always thought she was more likely to be a—you know—re-cruiter."

"Recruiter?"

"For another organization. I thought she might have been sent here to get to know the staff."

"I see." Christian paused, at a loss for words. Was that a smirk forming on Slater's face? He'd like to give him something to smirk about.

"Of course, if you insist, I can follow up with Human Resources, but like I said—"

"I heard you. If there's any follow up, I'll take care of it myself."

"Look, don't get me wrong. I'll do whatever you want—"

"It's all right. I'll take care of it."

He deserved an explanation. She might not feel the same way he did. But he deserved to know why she had left so abruptly, without saying goodbye or attempting to get in touch. She owed him that much. Perhaps the explanation would be perfect. She had feared to intrude on his grief. But now nothing stood in the way. Nothing.

He could see the thin white arms opening to him as he crossed the street and entered the vestibule of the apartment building. He found her name, just as he remembered, Lemereaux, printed in Gothic script on a little white card. He pressed the bell.

"Yes?" a woman's voice sounded raspy and far away through the intercom.

"Julie?"

"Who is this?" the intercom answered.

"It's Christian."

"And you want to see Julie?" or something like that. The sound was cutting in and out.

"Yes, Juliette Lemereaux."

"One moment," there was a long pause, as though she were conferring with someone, then the sound of the buzzer. He went inside and climbed the stairs to the second floor. He recognized the striped carpeting, even the dust in the corners of the hall. A man stood on the landing. He wore a pair of pants with the suspenders dangling as though they had been hastily pulled on and a long undershirt. His thick dark hair was touseled as though he had risen from his bed. "I am Auguste Lemereaux," he said in a thick French accent. "What is it that you want with my daughter?"

"Your daughter—that can't be?"

The man cocked his head and raised an expressive eyebrow.

"I'm sorry but the Julie I'm looking for is my age, petite and very blonde."

"Someday perhaps. The Juliette Lemereaux who

lives here is four years old. She is sleeping as was I when you rang our bell."

"Would you mind if I came inside?" he called wildly as the man returned to his own doorway, "only for a minute, just to see. I was here, you know, I remember this place."

"Go home, Monsieur. Someone is playing a trick." The dark wood door closed behind him. The hall was a succession of these doors all staring disapprovingly at Christian as he turned and went back down the stairs.

He went back to the lab because he couldn't think where else to go. The elevator sounded unusually loud in the deserted building. Even the cleaning crews were gone. He had seen their truck leaving the parking lot as he pulled in. The lights were on movement sensors that lit bank by bank, announcing his presence as he made his way through the darkened halls. Slater was still hanging around. He could see him as soon as he turned the corner, immersed in some files, his desk an island of light in the shadowy room. He looked up startled as the lights came on.

"I thought I was the only one here." He smiled until he saw the look on Christian's face.

"Where is she?"

"Who? What are you talking about?"

"No more bullshit." Christian grabbed at his lapels. He was amazed at the ease with which he pulled the big man to his feet. Slater made no resistance at all. Or maybe it was just that Christian had developed the strength of the insane. "You know who I mean! Julie—Juliette Lemereaux."

Slater eased himself out of Christian's grip and stepped back. "Are you crazy?"

"No, I'm not," Christian was back in his face. "Although I might think that I was, after that little setup tonight."

"I don't know what you're talking about. I told you everything I knew about that girl when you asked me. I don't know anything more. Zip! Nada!"

"You don't think I believe that story you told me about the agency!"

"I guess I can't help whether you believe it or not. Look, will you step back—?"

"We don't work with agencies. Working with agencies is dangerous in our business. Even you are smart enough to know that. In fact that's all a guy like you does know. How to keep two steps ahead of the competition. How to save your ass. Was there something between you? Is that what I missed? Were you dumb enough to make a play for her and did she turn you down? Is that why she had to go?"

"Look, Christian, I'm going to appeal to your reason if you have any left. The girl was nothing to me. Just a mistake that I made. First me and then you, apparently."

That was when Christian hit him, so hard that he felt as though he had broken his hand. Slater wasn't expecting it. He staggered and then fell against the wall. "You've got it all wrong. That's not what I meant—" There was blood coming from Slater's nose but Christian was too far gone to care. He came at him again with all his strength.

But Slater saw him coming. Dazed as he was and bleeding, he side-stepped the punch and seized Christian by the shoulders. It was as though he had just remembered how strong he was. In a minute their positions were reversed. Slater lifted him into the air. Christian was pinned against the wall with his feet dangling.

"Don't hit me again!" he shouted very slowly into Christian's face. "You had your fun now let it alone."

Christian squirmed like a bug. "Hit me back then, why don't you? Fight like a man!"

"Hit you?" Slater roared, "I'd like to kill you, you son of a bitch."

"Then why don't you? Put me down and let's fight."

"Because it's worth my job. You'll probably have me fired anyway because of this crazy business about the girl."

"Me have you fired?! Put me down," he shrieked.

"Promise you won't hit me again?"

Christian reared back with all his strength but he couldn't budge. Slater's grip was like iron.

"Promise?" Slater shook him like a doll and for one terrible minute Christian was afraid he would burst into tears. Then slowly the big man lowered him to his feet and began straightening his clothes. "You have to promise you won't run at me again like that. It's not fair. I can't fight back."

Christian snorted. "Why not?"

"As if you didn't know. I'm going to turn my back now and you've got to promise not to—"

"I promise, but I don't understand why you can't just fight back."

"I know you think I'm an asshole, but I'm really just an ordinary guy trying to survive, that's all."

"Survive what?"

Slater looked at him a long time before he answered. "The word is that you're extremely well connected."

"Connected to what?

"I don't know. I only work here and I'd like to keep on working here, if you don't mind. So let's just pretend that tonight never happened."

"What are you talking about?"

"Listen, if I knew where the girl was, I'd get her for you, believe me. I'm supposed to take good care of you, to make sure you have everything you want."

"Why?"

"Why do you think?"

Christian blinked.

"That's right," Slater laughed. "You're the fair-haired boy and somebody's got very big plans for you."

SIX

The key turned easily in the lock. His mother's kitchen was as clean as he had ever seen it. A few motes of dust dancing in a beam of afternoon light. A single glass draining upside down on the sink. Joszepa must have come on schedule. He would have to remember to call her. Maybe she would help him dispose of his mother's belongings. Maybe she herself would like some of the clothes. He briefly pictured the elderly Polish woman in one of his mother's caftans with the moon and stars pendant around her neck and the matching earrings. Maybe not. But at least she would clean out the closets.

He passed through the living room to the front hall where the staircase ran up to the second floor. This was the moment he had been dreading. He swept up the stairs without stopping not giving himself time to think. There was still a faint whiff of scotch. He stopped on the landing to pull the window open. Children were playing in the yard next door. Still. Tess had heard them every day while she worked.

The room at the top of the stairs had become her study when he moved out. Still it felt strange to open the door just at this time of day with the house so quiet all around him, as though he had just come home from school. His mother would be working in her own room. She would call out to him when she heard him on the stairs. She tried to sound cheerful, but Tess had never been an early riser so she was just getting started by the time Christian came home each afternoon. He could sense her impatience even as she called to him. "Christian, is that you?" Already? It seems like you just left. So he learned to cut his stories short.

"Give me a kiss. Then go downstairs and get some fruit. Be a good boy and play quietly until I finish this/ start this/ fix this . . . story/poem/article/letter." Sometimes he made her a cup of tea. "That's my good boy," she would say, as he carried the saucer with both hands, careful not to slosh. But just as often she wouldn't notice, too deeply engrossed in her work to even look up when he entered the room.

The room was just as she had left it. Her reading glasses lay on the blotter next to a sheaf of papers. Her sweater still hung on the back of the chair. He studied the snapshots in their plastic frames. Christian himself in a black snowsuit with a yellow stripe standing in the front yard with one arm around a giant snowman. Tess and Lena when they were young. Grandma and Grandpa's wedding picture. Christian in his cap and gown, squinting into the sun.

The one that interested him the most was buried deep in a bottom drawer. A young man in sun glasses wearing what might have been army fatigues. It was hard to tell. The boy had taken his shirt off, not from vanity, it looked as though he had been working and stopped a moment for the photograph. Was Tess holding the camera or one of his buddies? Had the picture been taken on a military base somewhere? In the jungle? Or was this just a kid from the neighborhood where Tess had grown up? Somebody digging a vegetable garden in the summer of 69.

The pants were dark. They could have been fatigues or just dark pants. Or he could have been one of the thousands of boys who wore army fatigues as a sign of general militancy and disrespect for the system. He would have looked better with a beard. Even a scraggly one would have marked him as a poet, a young Pan in charge of his life. Instead he looked like a boy trying to prove himself, trying to be what the patriarchy called a man.

The strongest argument for the military was the length of the boy's hair. That and the feeling Christian had that it was the decision to become a soldier that had separated them, had led his mother to bury the picture in the bottom drawer. A soldier might be loved and even longed for, but he could never be acknowledged, not by the girl with her fist raised under the hand-painted banner. "Huelga!" Tess had told him that it meant strike. The picture had been taken at a rally for Cesar Chavez and his farm workers in the 60's.

She was very forthcoming with the details of those

times, the miles they had marched, the indignities suffered at the hands of the Pigs and even her own family. Her father had called her a "hoor," mispronouncing whore in a way that had made her laugh in his face and then cry, later on when she was alone, realizing that it was not "whore" that he had pronounced, but "hoor," a secret word, dwelling deep in his consciousness, a word he had never said aloud until the day he hurled it at his own daughter.

They were sitting at dinner in the kitchen of the house that had no air conditioning. Sweat was pouring from his grandfather's face, running down his chest, staining his Stanley Kowalski undershirt, the badge of the working man. His only child, his beloved daughter, the smartest girl in her class, had told him she was traveling to Woodstock, traveling in a Volkswagen van that was decorated with flowers.

No need to tell him she was sleeping with the driver. Grandpa had known from the way she carried herself, the air of defiance that made her suddenly too big for the little kitchen. He had known from her rolling hip-swinging walk that his daughter was now a woman. The same urge that had carried him from Mt. Carmel High School where he was the editor of the student newspaper into the steel mills where he worked like an animal. This same urge that had domesticated him utterly was carrying her away beyond his reach in a bus painted yellow and covered with flowers.

Tess was very forthcoming. She told him of the war between the generations. Of her pain and of her father's pain that she had come to know too late. She told Christian everything except what he most longed to know.

Who his father was. Who *he* was, really. And why he was so different from his bold, risk-taking mother. She was so beautiful, so full of hope and energy. The boy in the picture looked thoughtful and withdrawn. His chest was thin and under-developed. On the day he found the picture, so long ago, he must have been 11 or 12, Christian had taken off his own shirt and stood staring at himself in the bathroom mirror, frowning and flexing his muscles.

He sat down in his mother's chair behind the el-shaped teakwood desk she had bought at a house sale. The desk that he remembered was nothing more than a door mounted on two trestles. She had an IBM-Selectric in those days. Christian had been fascinated by the balls that could be lifted on and off to change fonts. Letter Gothic was his favorite. Now she had a computer with an enormous double monitor and a stand to hold her notes at eye level while she typed.

She was doing quite well for herself. It must be those stories she had published. Women's fiction they called it. Romance with just enough history to make it respectable. He could never bring himself to finish one of her books, even though he was so proud of her. They were so utterly implausible and betrayed an ignorance of men and their motives that was embarrassing.

His mother was 50 years old. What had she been doing all those years that she still didn't understand the opposite sex? Or maybe she just enjoyed romanticizing life. She didn't want to know men at all. She wanted to idealize them, to alternately worship and despise them in her overblown florid prose while all the time her heart longed for a skinny boy with a hairless chest who had died at Khe Sanh or Da Nang before Christian was born.

Or had he come back? Christian wondered about all the years that stretched between himself and the boy in the photograph. Was he living now? Had they stayed in touch without Christian knowing, without his grandfather or anyone in the family being aware? How had she supported him all those years? She had never had a "real" job, not as far back as he could remember. Brief periods of telephone sales and even a light brush with real estate but never a real job, never a job that you left the house for.

Perhaps Grandpa helped. He pictured the stony silence between them, Grandpa tight-lipped and frowning, his mother chatting gaily pretending not to notice and Christian trapped between them in the kitchen of the little house, trying to cut his meat by himself, lifting the glass of milk with both hands, praying that no one would notice, that he would be carried safe in the eye of the storm. Had his mother's life long rebellion that she flaunted like a brightly colored scarf been financed by a man in a sweat-stained undershirt, a foreman in the steel mills?

Or had there been another source? The boy in the photograph? Christian realized that his hand was shaking. He took hold of the drawer pull and slowly, very slowly, began to slide it open. He knew just where the photograph was. He could see it looking up at him, so clearly, that for a moment, the fact that it was no longer there failed to register. She must have moved it. He searched through the contents of the drawer, finally pulling it out and dumping it on top of the desk. Then the other drawers, one by one, systematic at first and then frantic.

He found a plastic box of floppy disks. He flipped through them idly. And some file cards with story ideas on them. Her Rolodex was still open to Helen Carver's address and phone number in Manhattan. Her calendar read October 31, 1997. She must be tearing the old pages out and using them to write notes. Her appointment book lay open to the correct date. He saw his own name scrawled across the whole of Sunday afternoon and museum written on the line for 2:00 p.m. The concert was written in for Saturday night. Friday was blank except for a faintly penciled H? at 1:30 and below that a telephone number.

He was reaching for the phone when he noticed the concert tickets stuck in the corner of the blotter. He pressed the memory dial for Lena. The soft brogue answered. "Lena, did my mother ask you to go to a concert with her last Saturday?" He heard the faint sucking noise on the other end. Lena was smoking again. "It's me, Christian," he added.

"I know it's you. How is my poor Lamb?" she crooned.

"Lena, did my Mother ask you to hear Shostakovich? I gave her my ticket."

"No, darling, she didn't."

"Did she have plans to go with anyone else? Do you know?"

"I wish I could say that I did. Why?" she added after a pause and another puff. "Is it important?"

"I found the tickets on her desk. I told her to take you. Until this minute I assumed that she had."

"Are you at your mother's place now, Lamb?"

"I'm cleaning out her desk or trying to. Lena—?"

"Are you by yourself?"

"She made me her literary executor, you know."

"No, I didn't." Her voice hinted at disapproval.

"Helen told me. It was what she wanted."

Lena tsked softly.

"Lena, there's something I need to know. Did she—I mean I remember from before, when I was little but did she, now, I mean—"

"Precious Lamb, what is it?"

"Did she have a boyfriend? Was she dating anyone?"

"You know you were her darling boy, Christian, the center of her life just as she was of yours—"

"Lena, I need to know. Could there have been a man here with her on the night she died, someone that she might have invited to the concert."

"It's too soon for you to be sitting alone in that empty house, thinking God knows what—"

"Lena, you don't understand."

"I want you to go downstairs this very minute and get yourself a nice cup of tea. I was your mother's closest friend. I'm speaking to you now with her voice, saying what she would say . . . "

"A man who drank scotch—"

"A scotch drinker?" She was probably drinking some herself. Her brogue was getting thicker. He remembered driving her home one night. It was like having Barry Fitzgerald in the back seat. "Not that I recall . . ."

"Someone who's name began with H?"

"Haitch?"

"It's all right, Lena. It doesn't matter."

"I've been meaning to call you, but I've been so down myself. What are we going to do without her, Christian?" He could hear the tears in her voice.

"I don't know, Lena. I'm sorry I bothered you."

"It's always a pleasure to hear your voice, Christian. You remember that. If you need anything."

"I will."

"And go on home now. It's too soon."

"The house has to be sold. I have to go through her things."

"Then wait until we can do it together. Promise me. . ."

"There may be business associates of my mother's that I should contact. People who aren't aware—"

"That's Helen's job. Let her do what she's paid for. Taking 20% out of your mother for as long as I knew her."

"Twenty percent? I thought that 15 was the standard rate, even 10, but never—." He decided to carry on in this way for a while. It would do Lena good. He could hear the strength coming back into her voice.

"That's what I told your mother, but you know her, she was loyal. It's a two-way street I used to say to her. You wouldn't believe what she paid for health insurance—"

He forced himself to listen, murmuring patiently, while the second hand swept around once, twice, three times. Then he allowed himself to interrupt. "Lena, I think I'd better go."

"All right, Lamb, but don't forget about that tea."

"I won't."

"And Christian, put those papers in a box, if you must, and take them away with you. Promise me."

"All right, Lena. I'm getting kind of tired anyway." He yawned loudly. "I didn't sleep at all last night."

"Of course, you didn't. As close as you two were. And Christian, you were the light of her life, never forget that."

"I won't, Lena. Thanks."

"I'll call you soon. We'll have dinner."

"I don't know." Lena was a terrible cook. "I'm awfully busy these days at work."

"I'll call you. Take care of yourself, Christian."

"You, too, Lena. Bye."

He sat for a while staring at the teak bookshelves. They were jammed with books, two rows deep on some shelves. And all his mother's notebooks stacked in piles against the wall. He rubbed his eyes. Lena was right. He'd take his mother's diary so he could check her appointments. The rest he would leave for another day. But first . . .

He reached for the phone with one hand while with the other he turned the diary back to the tentative H and the phone number beside it. He punched it in quickly before he could change his mind: 737-8260. Two short rings and a man's voice answered. "Yes?"

Christian hesitated. "Who—who is this?"

The line went dead.

SEVEN

He was in the simulation room when he found it, a slight hesitation, a whisper of delay. The system paused, only for a moment, as though it had taken a long deep breath and needed more time to exhale. What is it? he wondered. Who's there? He shivered, feeling a draft, as though a door had been left open in the air-tight sound-less room. He stopped, waiting for the sound of spectral knocking or a message lightly tapped on the keyboard. That's how it would be on the eve of the 21st century. There were no more Ouija boards. The ghost would have to be in the machine.

Could his mother see him now sitting in his own lab, a secretary posted outside to guard the door. You've been working too hard, she would have told him. You should go home and change. Yes, you should very defi-nitely change, Christian. He scratched the stubble on his chin and smiled. He could almost hear her. You should get a life. He had been working too much lately. Maybe the hesitation he felt, that slight blink, was in him and not the computer at all.

He was testing doomsday scenarios, writing little code statements that would attack the records of a hypothetical company at various points in the processing cycle, just as Gartner had suggested. First, he simulated the dangers from within. Suppose the ordering system goes down, confused by the new array of dates. The bill of materials would be caught in an endless loop, like the sorcerer's apprentice, demanding the same parts over and over from the first level and ignoring the second and the third. Then there were the dangers from without, moving in ever widening circles through the supply chain. The funds that went untransferred, the payments that lagged, the interest that was never compounded.

Use your imagination, they had told him, push the envelope. He had tried to be cautious at first, scientific, until he realized that nothing would go to waste. Even if the results were not technically useful, they could still be used by the marketing department.

Sometimes Christian wondered why the clients didn't take matters into their own hands. Why didn't they just reset the dates on their own computers and run in parallel. They could do it at night after everyone went home. Or they could lease a few more computers. How expensive could it be? Certainly, not any more than the daily rates of the Doomsday Group.

If they set their systems ahead to the same date in the year 2000 and re-ran the day's work, they would have a foolproof test of the effects of the Millennium on their own operations. Why did no one ever think to do that, he wondered. Maybe they'd find out that there was no Y2K problem. Instead they preferred to hire Christian to sit all night in a soundproof room, imagining disasters and testing them across seventeen computers networked together to represent the world's major time zones.

"The Wave" they called it in marketing. All the salesmen had the demonstration installed on their laptops. It showed the Millennium as a beam of light moving westward across the map. Like a tropical storm powered by the force of 24 separate time zones, the salesmen told them, the Millennium would whirl around the globe, leaving devastation in its wake until it finally blew back out to sea and dissipated somewhere in the middle of the Pacific.

This was a very dramatic idea, one that sold a lot of maintenance plans as the clients envisioned a chain of disasters circling the globe. Christian himself couldn't decide if it was better or worse to have the new century happen in hourly increments. If pressed, he supposed he would have to come down on the side of marketing. The earth really was a small planet. The potential for new disasters bumping into older ones and accelerating geometrically could not be ignored.

He yawned just as the printer came on. He would make another pot of coffee. The girl—this week her name was Polly—had gone home hours ago. He could plug in his electric shaver. That would make him feel better. There'd be time to shave while he looked over the results. If everything turned out all right, he could go home, pick up a sandwich at the all-night deli. There was still time to crash, for a few hours at least, before he was due back in again in the morning.

Oh, Christian, he could hear Tess clucking, see her shake her head. It's just for a little while, he told her, until I get established. This is a once in a lifetime opportunity, once in a hundred lifetimes. The last time we changed Millenniums, Leif Ericson was discovering America. You should have stayed around, he really wanted to say, if you wanted to take care of me you should have stayed around. She disappeared then, still shaking her head, her eyes a deep well of unutterable sadness, so that he longed to call her back. To tell her he was sorry. She had done the best that she could. He knew that, had always known it.

Is that you, Tess, he asked as he glanced over the first pages of his report. Are you the ghost in the machine? Then he frowned as the printout claimed his full attention. The results were off in one of the hypothetical locations. The rubber plant in Caracas seemed to be running behind the bank in Manhattan that had wired funds for the payroll. That was odd. SA Western Standard Time was the same as Eastern Standard Time in the US. The two operations should be in synch. He sat down at the Caracas terminal and input the master codes. When he opened the Date/Time display on the control panel, he could see that the rubber plant was still running in 1999. For some reason the time change hadn't registered.

And then while he was watching, the little hour glass popped on the screen to indicate that an operation was running. The lights that showed he was powered up and networked, that files were passing from the terminal through the server and then back again began to blink.

Something was running? What? While he watched, the date changed to the year 2000.

Christian shook his head. That was the trouble with networks. Even when the telephone lines were all in the same room. There was no accounting for individual speeds and no guarantee of synchronicity. The program ran through the network at its own pace or at the pace of each individual workstation. If they experienced delays when the equipment was all in the same room, imagine what would happen when the installations were at a distance.

And there was always the idiot factor. Was there a chance that the resources needed to make the change would be competing with the billions of private citizens telephoning around the globe just at midnight to wish their friends and relatives a Happy New Millennium? The change in time zones didn't matter. The wave of consumer demand would follow the Millennium. Wherever the resources were most needed, that's where the overload would be. How could they test a thing like that? Did the telephone company have the answer? And if they claimed that they did, could he believe them?

Christian scrubbed his face with his hands. The stubble was gone but not the cobwebs in his brain, the acid churning in his stomach. Should he load the backup and rerun or accept the glitch as an isolated condition? He already knew the answer. The point of a test was not to "pass," but to find out where you were vulnerable, to study the interdependencies of your own programs, to follow the trail of "if . . . then's" until you figured out a way not to eliminate the dangers—that was impossible—but to compensate for them.

Accidents happen, so frequently and with such regularity that they hardly deserve the name accidents. Sure as there were rainstorms, there would be breaks in the line, places where moisture seeped into the network. In dry climates it was the dust itself— the tiniest particle—that would interfere with a circuit. The wise virgins brought extra oil. They probably had extra lamps, too, and backup bridegrooms.

Christian ran the test again and again. He ran it all night, always with the same results. . . almost. The hesitation persisted but it seemed to be moving at random from one workstation to another. Usually it consisted of a delay in moving from the old to the new year. But in Abu Dhabi at a remote desert station, he had seen the change reverse itself from 2000 back to 1999 and then on to 2000 again while he watched in worried fascination.

What is it? He asked himself as he paced the lab shortly before dawn. Outside the sky was streaked with light and the birds were beginning to sing. But here in the lab it was always midday, with plenty of coffee and fluorescent light to maintain the illusion. And then at 6:15, he noticed another variable. The closer he moved to December 31, the longer it seemed to take the computer to make the change, the more likely that two or even three workstations would be running behind the others. But when he moved farther out, by setting the computer back, say to January of last year and then resetting it to 2000, there was no lag whatsoever that he could see or if there was, it was evenly distributed throughout the network.

What kind of glitch was it that made it harder to advance the time the closer it got to the actual day that the time was supposed to advance? Think, Christian. Outside the soundproof steel door, the employees of the Doomsday Group were assembling for another day. He couldn't hear them but he sensed them occasionally passing by the door. And if he looked up, he would sometimes see a shadow in the reflecting glass.

At 9:30 when he had tried everything he could think of, he telephoned Slater. "I need you in the lab," he said with no preamble.

"I'm in the middle of—"

"Now!" he rasped, "I've found something unaccountable in the—"

"Don't say it! Not over the phone. I'll be right there."

In fifteen minutes Slater's head appeared in the window. Christian buzzed him in. "What took you so long?'

"I'm sorry."

The man was calm and well-dressed. He was wearing expensive cologne. Christian had been up all night, he reeked of coffee and sweat and his nerves were shot. " I asked you to come right away—I—"

"I came as fast as I could. I had to put some files away and lock them up. I couldn't leave them out—"

Christian put up his hand. "What—what did you say?"

"I had to lock up some personnel files. That's confidential information, you know. I couldn't just—"

There it was. The answer he had been fighting all

night. It wasn't an accident or a glitch. The system was doing something behind the scenes. Something that Christian could only guess at. And it needed additional time to put back the files and tidy up, to cover its tracks. "I think—" Christian began and then he took a deep breath. No point beating around the bush, not with someone as thick-headed as Slater. He wouldn't get it. Christian squared his shoulders. "We have a virus."

EIGHT

He had made a mistake. He should never have told him. It was too soon. He should have waited until he had more information, run more tests. Instead he had laid all his cards on the table. He had put himself in Slater's hands. Now all he could do was wait.

Slater shifted in his chair. Crossed his legs. Studied his finger nails. Finally he looked up. "It's impossible," he said.

Christian took a deep breath and tried again. "Listen," he said, "I've been here all night-"

"I know." Slater put up his hands. "You need to get some rest. You're—you're—overwrought. We'll get someone else to run the programs. On second thought, we'd better keep this to ourselves. No sense getting anyone else all worked up. You go home and rest. When you come back tomorrow the problem will still be there. You can run the programs again yourself."

"What kind of a response is that?"

"Excuse me—?"

"I tell you that we have a virus and you tell me to take two aspirin and call you in the morning?"

"I really think that under the circumstances—"

"What circumstances—"

"I'm doing what I think is best for all of us."

"You're stalling. Why are you stalling?"

"All right." Slater pulled a wafer thin cell phone from his inside pocket. "Here." he said, extending the phone to Christian. "Press 1 for Mr. Gartner. But I really think the conversation will go better with a little more sleep and a lot more evidence."

"Now you're bluffing!"

"Why would I do that?"

Christian couldn't say. But he knew stalling when he saw it, just as he knew there was something wrong with the system, even if he couldn't yet put his finger on the problem.

"Listen, Christian." He was standing too close, insinuating himself into Christian's space. "I'm on your side! Hieronymous Gartner isn't the man you go to unless you have all your facts straight. Especially not with something as serious as this."

"But there is no way to "get the facts straight," as you put it," Christian mimicked. "You can't see a virus like this. You only know it's there by inference. It's like a shadow that dogs your steps or—" he reached for an image that Slater would understand—"or a bomb!" That was it! He could see that he had hit home. "You can hear it ticking but you don't know where it is or when it's set to go off."

"So what do you propose?"

"I don't know," Christian scrubbed his face with his hands. "You're right about one thing. I am exhausted. But one more day isn't going to buy us any more information than we already have."

"No, but it will buy you a little sleep and the chance to come up with a plan. Listen, if I call Gartner now, he'll have the whole think tank here in forty minutes. This place will be swarming with chipheads—all of them brilliant enough to have an idea and too well paid to actually work on it. They'll be shouting out orders a mile a minute. That will be the last sleep you get for the rest of the week."

"All right then, I guess we'll do what you say. But I can't get over the feeling that you're stalling."

"I know," Slater said, with a crooked little smile. "But I'm not. We're on the same side, Christian. Honest"

Slater had put him out of his own lab. Turned him around and walked him to the door like a salesman without an appointment. Christian raised the weight bar over his head. It was hard to remember when to exhale. Pushing the air out of your lungs at the moment of greatest strain went against his instincts. But he felt like he was getting the hang of it. Up, down, up, down . . . up! The man on the treadmill was pretending not to stare. Was he making noise? Groaning as he pushed up with all his force and then sighing with relief as he brought it down. God, this was good! As good as sex . . . better! That guy better quit staring if he knew what was good for him.

All the managers of the Doomsday Group were members of the Lakeside Athletic Club. It was one of the perks that raised them a notch above the hackers sitting all day in front of their monitors. Slater had pressed his card on him as he propelled him toward the door.

"Go on," he insisted, his hand on his shoulder, his voice close to his ear, whispering encouragement. "Sit in the steam, lift a little, maybe go for a swim. You'll feel like a new man." Christian was too busy dodging his minty breath to refuse.

"Off you go now," he gave Christian a little shove when they reached the door. Christian whirled around just in time to prevent a playful tap on the ass. He clenched his fist but Slater was oblivious. "I'll call ahead; tell them you're on your way."

The Club was a block square and four stories high. There were tennis courts on the roof, a pool and a sun deck. In the summer they set up a portable bar and grilled brats and chicken breasts. Inside there were weight rooms and running tracks, studios for aerobics and Jazzercise, a spin room. There were restaurants and a boutique that specialized in exercise clothes. You could go in at 9 in the morning and emerge at midnight without feeling you had wasted your day.

It was a great place to meet girls, a little city of lean, health-conscious singles, with here and there some dedicated middle-agers who worked out and minded their own business and the occasional family—couples who had met in the juice bar, married on the roof garden and now couldn't resist coming back with their toddlers dressed in matching exercise suits. For people like this, there was a nursery so they could drop off their kids while they ran off to class.

Christian climbed the steel stairs to the registration desk. It was lunch time and people streamed up and down the stairs. They pushed past him toting gym bags or wearing sweats under their expensive downtown coats. Most of them seemed to know each other. All the girls had highlights in their hair and most of the men wore suits. He had to make his way around chatting attractive couples and people talking on cell phones.

There were four people behind the big wooden desk, checking credentials and buzzing the chosen through the big wooden door. Everything else was glass so you could see what you were missing while you waited in line. The girl who waited on Christian was wearing a black lycra halter and chewing gum. Her hair was teased and pulled into a big off center pony tail that made Christian want to fix it the same way your eye is drawn to a crooked picture on the wall. She wore a terry cloth sweat band around her forehead and another on her wrist.

"Aren't you cold?" he asked, just to make conversation while she looked over the pass that Slater had given him. She made no answer, just eyed him strangely while she pressed some buttons on the phone. She had long colorful fingernails, the kind associated with ancient Chinese dynasties rather than exercise clubs. Christian felt sorry for her. He wouldn't have been able to put together a credible outfit himself but he knew when he saw one that didn't work. Her shopping mall chic branded her an outsider as much as Christian who had no outfit at all. He didn't see why a girl would choose to dress like that and stand in a drafty hallway checking IDs, but whatever her reason, it wouldn't work. In a year or two she'd be back in the discount store where she belonged.

The person on the other end of the phone must have told her something that surprised her. She broke into a big smile. "Mr. Slater called about you," she beamed as she pressed the buzzer. The members were allowed to go straight in but guests were given forms to fill out on little clipboards. Then they were herded into another line and taken one by one into little booths where they were grilled about their income and "personal objectives." The terminology puzzled Christian until he realized that they really wanted to know how much weight you wanted to take off or if you were here primarily for strength training and maintenance or even social reasons. The personal objectives were easy he realized when he glanced at the form. You could choose them from a list.

He didn't have to bother anyway. Someone gave him a clipboard. Then someone else appeared carrying a brand new set of sweats purchased just for him in the gift shop. There was a whispered conference with a lot of frowning. The person who had given him the clipboard was explaining that he didn't know—"how was I supposed to know?" as they pulled Christian out of line and hurried him upstairs.

Slater really had called. He was not to be harassed about membership or forced to fake some kind of metaphysical statement about the place of exercise in his life—

he had pretty much decided on mens sana in copore mensa but he thought that "lifto ergo sum" would look better on a tee shirt. Instead he was taken directly to the weight room—the executive one on the third floor that you needed a keycard to get into—where his own personal trainer—"Jared" he had identified himself, extending a beefy hand—weighed him in and showed him how to operate the Nautilus.

"We'll start low, let's say forty," Jared ran a practiced eye over Christian's body. He never worked out but he was naturally thin and he suspected that tension was actually good for muscle tone. When his arms began to shake, Jared made a quick adjustment. "Don't push too hard," he said as he pulled off first a 10 and a then a 5 pound weight. "Good form is more important than weight or speed."

"Why is Slater doing this?" he thought as he pumped, pushing up with all his force, trying to visualize his shoulders as the source of his power, then relaxing or trying to as he brought the bar down. The rhythm of his breathing was supposed to drive the exercise. Images of Slater drifted into his consciousness. He neither focused on them nor sought to drive them away. He let them rise up and float where they would like bubbles in a lava lamp.

What had Slater been doing on the night Christian found him alone in the office so late? The thought presented itself as a picture rather than a question. Slater surrounded by files, his desk an island of light in the darkened building. How surprised he had been to see Christian, how startled!

Christian tried to reconstruct the moment when

Slater realized he was not alone. His body betrayed the lapse of concentration and Jared was on him in a heartbeat. "Focus," he said, raising his own arms to mirror Christian's. And then again in a soothing, almost hypnotic voice, "Focus." Christian stopped trying, he let his body become a powerful column of air moving in and out, pushing the weights up and then bringing them down as easy and as inevitably as breathing.

He gave himself to the rhythm of the exercise, only gradually becoming aware that Slater's face was slowly materializing like a picture in a developer. He saw the crooked grin, the look of a boy caught reading after lights out. He saw what he had missed, that Slater had been preoccupied with the file he was reading. His need to close it quickly and shove it out of sight had slowed his response and made him docile and easy to handle.

And when he finally responded, it had been only to hold Christian back, to prevent the situation from escalating. Why was that? Because Christian held some kind of mysterious power? Of course, he was one of the Brotherhood of Chipheads, the mysterious force that would someday rule the earth. Guys with bad complexions who sat in their rooms all day surfing the net and playing with themselves, while dumb guys like Slater, guys with MBAs, ran all the companies and took home all the big paychecks.

The suits! The suits had done it to him again. Christian wanted to bang his head against the wall. Instead he used the force of his lament to push the weights as high as they would go. He had run with his information about the virus to the man who had probably planted the virus. No one could be as dumb as Slater seemed and work for a computer consulting firm. It was all an act and Christian had fallen for it, as had Hieronymous Gartner. He inhaled. If Gartner could be so easily fooled then there was no shame. He was in good company. And if he had the wit to play along, maybe it wasn't too late. Maybe he could still turn Slater's stratagem against him.

"Focus!" Jared was in front of him again. He stood there until Christian got his rhythm back, until he realized that he couldn't think, breathing was the only thought that his body had room for. But he could see a thought if it entered his mind as an image, the same way that images swirled through dreams, embodying messages from the unconscious.

He saw Mr. Gartner shaking his hand. Then the image dissolved and it was the boy in the picture that he saw. He had taken off his glasses and his eyes were just like Christian's. His chest swelled with pride and his muscles looked bigger and more defined. He looked directly at Christian and he smiled.

NINE

He stayed in the weight room for as long as he could, until Jared shook his hand and said that he was looking forward to working with him again. Then he made his way down to the steam room. He tried to keep the feeling of being centered in his own body. His walk seemed different, he rolled on the balls of his feet, his hips and shoulders swinging in unison like a well-oiled machine.

There was a small window in the door of the steam room. He could see mysterious figures shrouded in towels or lying naked on benches. He took a deep breath, pushed the door open and was engulfed in a swirling mist. For a moment he was disoriented. He stood too long in the doorway, trying to get his bearings.

Then someone made room for him on a bench and he sat down as quickly as he could. Someone else got up and poured more water on the rocks. Christian saw the hiss and felt the sweat beginning to bud. Just sitting made him edgy at first but gradually he gave himself up to the intense heat and the water rolling down his face and back. He took on the shrouded group identity of the steam room. He blended in, disappeared as a person with problems of his own and became one with the steam and with the row of naked sweating humanity.

He forgot about Slater and the virus. If he thought about it all, he imagined that it must be a great mistake, a misunderstanding that wasted his energy. The door was thrown open and he stared with annoyance until it finally closed. How rude the world was and how distracting. He looked down at his watch and tried to calculate the time he had spent in the steam. The next time the door opened, he got up reluctantly and pushed himself out into the cold.

He stood for a long time in the shower, letting the water stream over him and bring him back to life. Everything seemed new and different. He put on his clothes as though he had never seen them before, as though the face in the mirror belonged to another man, someone well rested and at peace with himself.

What should he do with this new relaxed identity? Where should he go? He began smiling at the people around him. Some people ignored him, perhaps they thought he was smiling at someone else. But others returned the smile as if they recognized him, as if he were a regular whom they had seen before even though they couldn't remember his name. "Hey!" someone called out jovially, another one asked how it was going.

He made his way downstairs slowly, savoring his new identity. He stopped at the snack bar in the lobby and ordered a bowl of soup and a pita filled with chicken salad. While he ate, he thought about going back to the office. It was only 6:30. Slater should be gone by now and he could get a jump on tomorrow's tests. The woman beside him at the counter was sipping herbal tea. She smiled and said that she loved it here and couldn't bear to go back out into the cold.

Christian smiled back, like a co-conspirator. Could the virus be the product of paranoia and loneliness? He thought about telling the woman next to him, just to hear what she would think, if the virus would seem real to her. They chatted for a while. When he paid for his meal, he felt his mother's keys in his pocket.

Outside the snow was just beginning, sifting down in big flakes, the kind that melted on your tongue. It was 7:30 but the holiday shoppers kept the rush hour going. The horns sounded good natured. He and the girl parted at the front door, wondering if it would snow all night and if the traffic would be bad in the morning.

He walked along, staring at the holiday windows. He couldn't go back to the office and shut himself in for another night. His apartment in Rogers Park seemed too far away, especially if the weather turned bad. The windows sparkled with little white lights. He saw an Iceland sweater and a scarf that his mother would have liked. Maybe he should have a tree, even though she was gone. It might make him feel better.

He let himself in quietly as he had so many nights before. The house was dark as though she were sleeping or out somewhere on her own. They always put the tree in the corner. He stood there a minute and measured the space with his hands. He could hear them arguing about the lights. Tess always waited until he was finished, until the tree was standing, encircled with lights, to make her suggestions.

"The lights are too far in!" she would lament. "I can't see them!"

"You should have been here while I was hanging them. It's too late now."

"Christian, really. They're just clinging to the tips of the branches! I can see all the wires!"

"You should get married," he told her, "so you can have a full-time handyman at your beck and call. I'm just passing through."

The decorations were upstairs in the attic. He knew just where they were. Last Christmas he had bought her a set of red and green rubber tubs with an intricate system of cardboard dividers. *"You're* the one who should get married, Christian," she told him while he placed each ornament in its cardboard nest, then rolled the tinsel garland neatly around itself and laid it carefully on top. "That kind of obsessiveness is wasted on a single man. It takes a woman to really appreciate it."

"You know I don't think you really enjoy the tree at all. You're too busy vacuuming up the needles. I know you don't like decorating it in the first place. You resist all my ideas, you're in too much of a hurry to get it up. But putting the ornaments away, that's your favorite part," she railed at him while he struggled to get the rubber tubs around the bend in the attic stairs.

The house was too quiet. He wandered upstairs, uncertain now why he had come. The door to his mother's room stood open. He stared at the white duvet and the pile of pillows, remembering the comfort of his mother's bed. Tess burned incense and aromatic candles and the room was dotted with dishes of potpourri. She changed scents regularly, at least once a month, sometimes more depending on how she felt. This one was fresh and sweet, peaches and vanilla, he decided, breathing deeply.

It was a big room. There was a chaise lounge near the window and a barrel table with a leather top that used to be downstairs in the living room. Books were everywhere, crammed into shelves against the wall or standing in piles on the floor. Sometimes her loom was up or the ironing board, depending on what she had been doing. When he was little he had begged to sleep in here. She had let him sometimes when he was sick or awoke frightened from a bad dream or a thunderstorm. She would prop him up against the pillows and sing him a song or read to him. Sometimes she held him stroking his hair absently with one hand while with the other she turned the pages of a book.

Too many ghosts, he decided, closing the door and tiptoeing softly into the hall, as though a sick person were inside, as though Tess herself were waiting there. With every breath he smelled not peaches and vanilla but Tess herself. The room reminded him of a time when he had loved his mother with a single-mindedness that frightened him, when he had seen her clearly as the source of his well-being, claimed her as his own, longed for the warmth of her body and her bed unselfconsciously and without shame.

He thought of all the books and the movies in which the ghost cannot rest because someone on earth is still holding on and refuses to release them. He remembered anecdotes of terminally ill people who could not die because their loved ones withheld permission, refused to let them go. Those must have been responsible people, not like his mother who had slipped away, stolen away like a thief in the night, just at the time when it would hurt him the most, when he had found a woman to love and needed her help and support to disentangle himself, to release the mother-son bond without tearing the flesh or destroying the tender shoots he still needed to bond with another.

She had died to get away from the confrontation that she knew was coming, had drunk too much brandy and then thrown herself down the stairs. Now he would never be free. He remembered watching *Wuthering Heights*, the two of them side by side on the old couch before she had it recovered, sharing a blanket and a big bowl of popcorn. Laurence Olivier as Heathcliff calling out to the dead Cathy, a strange name he had always thought for a 19th century character. It sounded like the name of one of his mother's friends. "Haunt me!" Heathcliff had cried, mad with grief. "Haunt *me!*" Even as a child, Christian had understood that wild and wrongful passion. Even as a child, his eyes had filled up with tears.

Her study was safer, the life of the mind more orderly and controlled. He always marveled at the neatness of her workspace. That and her penmanship. At 50 Tess still had the round open hand of a school girl. In college she had tried to make it look more artistic, the letters free and unconnected, calligraphic like Christian's own hand. But by then it was too late.

"You were taught to hold the pen loosely between your thumb and forefinger, with your middle finger poking out to brace it, but ever so lightly." Tess demonstrated. "Then you made a series of big open circles, like this, over and over, just to practice the technique. Then you were ready for the letters. While you worked, the nun would circulate, grabbing at the pen if she thought you were holding it too tight. That was supposed to help you relax, the fear of some crazy old woman in black pouncing on you." Tess had always held the pen too tight. Her middle finger was bent and callused. Her witch's finger, she called it. "I couldn't make the letters right unless I held it like that."

That was the secret that he kept for her, the thing he had observed while growing up. Tess might believe in all-night parties and free love—although he could not remember that she shared her bed with any male except himself—but she also believed there was a "right" way to do things, a way despite all her ideas that things were supposed to come out. This had more to do with Grandpa's workbench—where the screws and nails were sorted and kept in identical jars and the place where each tool fit was outlined on the wall—than it did with politics or the free and easy morals of the 60s.

He opened the notebook that still sat below her reading glasses on the teakwood desk. It was a simple ruled composition book with the date and the words *Y2K: The Scorpion Chronicles* written on the cover. She began all her projects this way, taking notes, jotting down ideas, researching topics just as the nuns had taught her. She railed against religion but Christian noticed that the older she got, the more she reverted to the habits of her girlhood. Good organization and round open penmanship. The Palmer Method, they had called it when Tess was in school.

The first few pages outlined the project she had described to Christian on the phone two days before she died. *Technology is evolving faster than the human mind can assimilate*, she had written. *We are set on a collision course with forces beyond our control. We are desperately in need of time to undo the damage done by entrepreneurs who feel that the responsibility to their stockholders outweighs their responsibility to the planet. Our ozone layer is eaten up by chemicals, our own immune systems compromised by antibiotics.*

Those who see the danger respond by taking better care of themselves, working out at the gym, eliminating fat from their diets, as though they could control in this way the course of a world gone mad. Meanwhile they run their air conditioners and drive their cars on congested freeways and live as though theirs was the only life worth saving, as though they had the right to thrive at the expense of the poor and the weak. Meanwhile the third world sells off the earth's remaining resources, to buy a share in the global economic games.

Zebulon is a high-ranking member of a secret society with a plan for turning technology against itself. " Zebulon? Oh Tess," he muttered, then resumed reading. *Named for the Scorpion who stings itself to death, the society has chapters all over the world—like the Masons—and they have been holding back the Millennium for centuries.*

There is evidence for the existence of the Scorpions in

the absence of certain basic kinds of records that we have written off as pre-historic. Why is there no extant version of the Iliad or Odyssey that can be traced directly to Homer. Why is there no real evidence for the existence of Homer himself or for the city of Troy? On a simpler note, why do people doing genealogical research have such trouble tracing their roots? Why can they find no record of the ports where their immigrant grandparents disembarked? Why in so many cases can they not find a reliable record of the grandparents themselves, no birth or marriage certificates, no records from the census?

Because civilization is really hundreds and thousands of years older than we imagine. Events that are assumed to have taken place in the last one hundred years are actually separated by a gulf in time so wide that it is amazing that any records have survived at all. Many people are amazed at the progress the world has made in the last 100 years, but the fact is that the last 100 years have been going on for centuries. Each time we approach the Millennium the Scorpions find a way to use our own technology to send us back in time.

They do this because they believe that sooner or later man's humanity will outstrip his technology, that we will learn not only to invent great things but to control them. There was great hope among the initiates for the hundred year period that is now drawing to a close, the 16th era as it is known among the Scorpions. (Since the term century is meaningless, the Scorpions refer to each period of one hundred years as an era. They have numbered these eras and recorded their histories so that if the world ever returns to real time, the history of those lost years can be recovered and the continuity and integrity of time may be restored.)

The realists know that this can never be. Like Macbeth,

the Scorpions have gone so far in blood that to turn back were the same as going on. But lately there is a movement among the young—much like the antiwar movement of the 60's—" Oh right, Tess!—to restore real time. Those who support this movement point to the excesses of the past era, claiming that instead of holding off disaster the Scorpion "manipulations" as they are politely termed are bringing us closer and closer to the brink.

That a great war cannot be avoided in the twentieth century is a known fact. The closing decade of the nineteenth century—a true century by the way whose time has never been manipulated—points clearly to such a conflagration. But that two such World Wars should occur with only a generation between them, just time enough to rearm and raise a new generation of soldiers, this was a new development, one that occurred only in the last era, and is held by the young Real Time Now! (RTN) Party as the strongest argument for disbanding the Society.

The Scorpions had arranged for the assassination of Archduke Francis Ferdinand to occur as early as possible—in prior eras he has lived to the age of 60 or even 75. Once he died before he could be assassinated. The First World War was delayed until 1953 and a nuclear holocaust avoided only by the narrowest of margins. They learned from that experience that the World War must occur as early as possible, for if the jingoism of the nineteenth century were ever to meet up with the technology of the twentieth, the world would surely come to an end. But if the conflagration occurs early in the twentieth century, when technology is still in its infancy, all out destruction can be averted.

Most important, the technology leading to the computer will be introduced and perfected in peacetime, so that society has a hope of mastering the electronic giant, the servant who so quickly becomes the master, before the century's end. But alas, who could have imagined Hitler? The world will be relieved to learn that this psychotic madman is a one time scourge, an unhappy coincidence and not a tradition. The next time around, he will succeed in his career as a house painter. Certain of the Scorpions are committed to making sure that there is an accident with the scaffolding.

The decision to catapult the world back in time is never made lightly. The Scorpions meet in solemn congress no earlier than 1985, no later than 1989, so that the fate of each era can be decided before it enters the last decade. That much time is needed to study the technologies of the day and to determine how the Event will be managed. This time the choice was easy. The shortsightedness of technicians in setting up the two digit year guaranteed a worldwide crisis that could be used by the Scorpions to their advantage.

The question of whether or not mankind can be trusted with his own future and the Scorpions disbanded at last is always hotly debated. This year the conservative faction used the two-digit year as proof that mankind would never be ready. But the RTN zealots argue that mankind has been so manipulated that the very notion of free will is at risk. "Mankind has not been allowed to remember," they argue as the story opens, "but we at least do not forget how long we have labored as the slaves of machines trained to accept 'the system requires or the system will not permit' as an excuse for the most blatant corporate chicanery."

"The habit of accepting a machine's parameters as the limits of our own inquiry has been bred into us for sixteen eras. During the same period, our environment has been fouled again and again with toxic waste and human experiment so that now *we see traces of radiation appearing earlier and earlier in each era and epidemics of cancer and other immune system diseases exploding on the horizon far ahead of schedule, before mankind has mastered anesthesiology and surgery, let alone the genetic engineering needed to shore up the immune system. We have transgressed against time itself, not once but over and over. How long before our transgressions seep into the nineteenth century and further weaken the gene pool that we seem dedicated to breeding out of existence?"*

In other words, the Scorpions have already failed in their mandate to protect society. As the story opens, Mara, Zebulon's consort and a leader of the RTN party, is arguing passionately for time to go forward. *"Wise and well-intentioned though we may be, we can only operate from hindsight. We dwell on the avoidance of past mistakes and miss the potential of the present moment. We have accepted blindly and made an article of our faith the Old Time adage that mankind will destroy itself in the twenty-first century. We fail to see that our own manipulations will be the agent and primary cause of this destruction. We are well-named, brothers and sisters. Our crimes will rise up to haunt us. In trying to foil the Oracle, we have bound ourselves, like Oedipus, ever more tightly in its coils."*

Christian closed the notebook. So this was what his mother had done with her idea. Not bad, except for the names and the speech at the end when she couldn't resist getting biblical or classical or whatever that was. But that was Tess for you. Give her the ball and she wasn't content to run with it. She wanted to levitate, to sail right over the goal post carrying the ball in her hand.

But this was good, this was way better than usual. What he liked best was that she finally had something to say about society. This was an appropriate message for a woman her age, not so Tess-centered and built on nothing more serious than romance gone wrong. The part about Hitler and Archduke Ferdinand was almost witty. Anyone would say so. Anyone would like this, all age groups, men and women. She was finally on a roll and the finished product should be commercially and artistically viable. He was really proud of her. So carried away with enthusiasm that he succeeded in forgetting for at least a minute, maybe more, that she was dead.

TEN

He was lying on the floor staring into the fire. He had found the old quilt in an upstairs closet and poured out the last of Tess's Courvoisier. "Here's to you, Tess!" He saluted the dancing flames. "You were a hell of a good mother and a fine person and a great writer especially at the end and I just wish I had the chance to tell you." Maybe there was something she wanted to tell him, too. He closed his eyes and waited.

When nothing happened, he decided to call his mother's agent in New York. He carried the telephone from the hall into the living room, cursing each time the cord stuck. Trust Tess to be out of step. A telephone in the hall was an idea left over from the 1930s, an era when people used the phone to give and receive brief messages. Judge Hardy had a telephone in the hall, directly under the staircase.

Everyone but Tess had a cordless phone. At least this one had a memory. Helen's name was opposite number 4. The telephone rang once and was answered by voice mail as he should have realized it would be. It was after 8:00. He was pretty certain he would find Helen's home number on Tess's Roladex and he did—under H instead of C. In a minute her clipped, almost foreign sounding voice was on the line.

"Helen! I hope it's all right to call you at home. This is Christian. Wahrmutter."

"I know! I'm so glad!" her voice was warmer and more spontaneous than he remembered. She sounded breathless and very young. "I mean, we have caller ID, and for a minute I thought, well,—"

"You thought my mother was calling you?"

"I did, actually, although I know that sounds strange."

"Not to me. I can feel her presence very strongly tonight. I need to talk to somebody who can, you know, who will—listen, is this okay? I don't know you very well but—"

"Of course it's okay. I miss her, too." Her voice was very soft.

"You know you're really a decent person," he blurted. "And however you felt about my mother and whatever you two did together, that's your business."

"What? What did you say, Christian? I think we have a bad connection."

"It's your own business and I'd say it to anybody. I could have called Lena but she drinks and it's getting pretty late. I was afraid I'd find her half in the bag, and you know, like they say in the bible, the last state of that man was worse than the first."

"Are you possessed by a demon tonight, Christian?"

"Very good! I see you're up on your biblical references."

"Maybe having a little something to drink yourself?"

"Maybe." Now he'd done it. Calling his mother's agent, someone that she did business with and insinuating that she was a lesbian. Except that lesbians didn't hide anymore, right? They had those parades.

"I feel kind of responsible."

"You do?" What was she talking about? He must have missed something.

"You tried to tell me that you didn't want to be her executor, that you couldn't handle it, but I pushed it on you anyway. I should have paid more attention to your feelings. Now it's late and you're alone and you're feeling overwhelmed . . ."

"Oh no—I mean it's late but I'm not overwhelmed. I'm just so damned proud. I never told her how proud I was and now it's too late." He couldn't help himself. He tried to swallow his sobs but they shook his body and he couldn't talk.

She was quiet for a long time, just listening, letting him cry. Tess always said what a great listener Helen was.

"Christian," she said at last, "are you still there?"

"I'm still here." He snuffled back his sobs. "I started reading her notes for the Scorpion Chronicles. And I realized how great she was, not just because she was my mother, but because of what she thought and who she was. It was the first time I saw her like that and I was so proud and the next minute I remembered she was dead. That was it. She'd never get a chance to finish this. Nobody but you and me would ever read it. And what was worse, I'd never have a chance to know this person that I'd just met, the person who lived in her work."

Helen didn't say anything but he thought that he could hear her crying, softly and unobtrusively, like a good agent, always in the background. He wondered what it was like on the other side of the line. What she was wearing and what her apartment looked like. Where the phone was, where she was sitting or lying right now and what kind of life she had.

"I loved her, too, you know."

"I know. What kind of house do you have? "

"Christian, listen to me. I loved your mother but we weren't lovers. I live with someone."

"Oh?"

"A man. His name is Ernest. He's a patent attorney. We have a very nice apartment overlooking Central Park."

"Good. I'm very happy for you."

"Ernest met your mother once, when she came into the city. We took her to the Met."

"I think she told me." Of course she hadn't or if she did, he hadn't been listening.

"Ernest sends his condolences."

"Thank you." They were probably lying on the bed, eating Chinese food out of little paper cartons and watching the news. That was New York, one big Woody

Allen movie. "Helen, I have one more question then I'll let you go."

"Ask anything you want, Christian. I'm not in a hurry. Ernest isn't even here. I'm just lying on the bed, reading."

He thought that she was lying down. Her voice had an intimate, prone quality. He wondered if Ernest really existed or she had made him up. "Well, I was wondering how far she got with this. If there was any chance that it could still be published, even if it was only in fragments."

"I'm not sure, Christian. I saw it about two weeks before she died. She told me that it was going well but I don't know that it was finished. You're in a better position than I am to know that."

"You said she sent it to you?"

"Yes, she e-mailed me the first 25 pages."

"Then it must be on her hard drive."

"Aren't you on line?"

"No, what I found was in one of her notebooks."

"Then you haven't looked in her documents folder?"

"No, I—" he felt a little embarrassed. "You see, she called me a few days before she died with some technical questions. The whole thing sounded crazy to me. I was watching a Bull's game and I kind of blew her off."

"So that's what's really bothering you." He could hear the relief in her voice. She really was a good person.

"I figured that she couldn't have gotten very far without me and I just wished that I had dropped what I was doing and gone over there when she called."

"Don't worry, Christian," Helen chuckled. "She found a way to solve her technical problems on the Internet."

"Tess on the Internet?"

"She said you showed her how to use it."

"Well, I did, but I didn't think she ever would. That wasn't Tess's style. She loved libraries, the smell of old books, losing herself in the stacks."

"This time she was in a hurry."

"Well, well, Tess on the Intenet. That's something else I didn't know about my mother."

"Don't be maudlin. She was having the time of her life. She died at the height of her powers, Christian. That's a loss for us but not necessarily for her."

"To die at the height of her powers?"

"To live at the height of her powers, Christian. Think of it like that, not the other way. Never to grow old, not really, or to wonder if she could still compete. She was just coming into her own."

He sighed.

"And there's something else. She said she'd met somebody."

He realized that he was holding his breath.

"Somebody who could help with her research."

"Did she say who it was? Did she mention a name?'

"No, but I had the feeling it was a man." He could hear her smiling. "Even though she didn't say. Something about the way she talked about him. Oh . . . and there was something else."

"Yes?"

"I think that he might have been someone she had known before. Somebody important who had come back into her life."

He had installed his mother's software and knew all her passwords, the machine itself was one that he had purchased for her. All she did was word processing and a little research. As a true bibliophile, she preferred books and paper but she claimed that the ease of technology was making her lazy. It was so much easier to surf the net than go to the library in search of primary sources. The library itself had been configured for on-line users. Most of the books were in storage. The stacks had been replaced by rows of computers.

He drummed his fingers on the desk as he waited for her machine to power up. A fragment of yellow protruded from under the computer. A pad of Post-It's with the address of the Doomsday Group in Tess's hand-writing. Christian smiled. She liked to look at the Staff Directory. It gave her pleasure to see him listed as an in-formation technology specialist. He had visited the site himself many times in the early days to gloat over his promotion. Then he had gotten used to it and so inun-dated with work that he had no time for surfing and no reason to gloat.

A snatch of elevator music and Windows 95 ap-peared on screen. He logged in and opened the web browser, using Tess's own passwords, the ones that he had set for her, based on the names of gods and goddesses, Zeus and Athena and Hera. He had been embarrassed be-yond belief to discover that all of her prior passwords had been variations of his own name, Cman and CJW and the simple but obsessional Chris38.

He worked quickly but couldn't avoid occasional brushes with his mother's screen saver. While the system worked behind the scenes, a picture of a haunted house filled the screen. A light went on in an upper window, a black cat scurried across the yard, the porch rocker creaked eerily, all the while a bat made its way across the night sky. When it had traveled from the far left to the far right of the screen, the display would begin again. The upstairs light would go on, the black cat would scurry, etc., etc., *ad infinitum*.

His mother had delighted in all these tricks, never realizing until he pointed it out—the spoilsport—that the special effects ran on an endless loop. "No?! Really?!" And that they were keyed to the passage of the bat across the screen. "My goodness, I think you're right. Just look at that!" The truly annoying thing was that she enjoyed them just as much and took to sharing her anticipation, "Watch now, the bat is almost past the chimney, the front door is going to creak open slowly and there'll be a scream. See that?" She would crow with delight, like a two year old.

The search engine opened and he typed in the address on the yellow Post-It: www.doomsdaygroup.com. The DDG logo assembled slowly on the screen and he scrolled through the options. The Staff Directory of course and the Directory of Services. Technology Briefs: The Journal of the 21st Century—that was a laugh—the only technology being briefed was the stuff that would lead to expensive new jobs for Doomsday. Then there was Malfunction Junction—full of Y2K horror stories—with an electronic form that would register you to learn more about SafeGuard 2000+—the Millennium Maintenance Plan.

Here was something he hadn't seen. Click here to visit our sister site: Highlights of the Twentieth Century. Come and play with us: Virtual 1900. Visit the major cities of the United States at the turn of the last century. Go shopping at the corner store and market, order from the Sears Catalog, drive a Model T on the roads your great-grandfather knew. All this and more: Click here to travel back in time to 1899. That must have been what Tess had been after. What better site for the author of *The Scorpion Chronicles* to do her research?

He clicked and clicked again, following her tracks back in time, to the days, just a few short weeks ago, although it seemed longer, when she had sat in this chair, a CD playing softly in the background—Faure—he had found it still in the player, even though he had warned her to return them always to their plastic jackets. "Hey buster," she had frowned, loving him for his neat, nerdy obsessions. "Who's the mother here?"

He spent the rest of the night in the world of his great grandfather, visiting the talking pictures, buying his shirts and celluloid collars at Chas. A. Stevens, stocking up on provisions, figuring the budget for a family of four. That made him wince. He could have spent a year at Yale for the money he earned in two days at The Group. He would have been a wealthy man, sitting on the wide front porch of a gracious home, boarding the train for the South Shore, his pockets bulging with suspicious looking money, the cartoon twenties dispensed by the local ATM, Andrew

Jackson leaping from the center of the bill, like Porky Pig stuttering "Th-th-th-that's all, folks !"

How long before he was arrested as a counterfeiter? But no! Virtual 1900 to the rescue. The money page supplied him with the names of collectors who could exchange his Lincoln pennies for Indian heads, his Roosevelt dimes for Lady Liberty. That would make a good Christmas present, he thought and scrolled far enough to see that the game had anticipated him. Twenty dollars worth of 1900 currency, along with a list of things it could buy, a night at the opera, followed by an intimate dinner at the Palmer House, and then a ride in a hansom cab back to your mansion on Prairie Avenue. You could even tip the driver. All this available for only $100, a collector's item, just in time for the last Christmas of the twentieth century.

His mother would have liked that. He bet that she had spent time here and at the Street Map of Old Chicago. Order your dream house from the Sears & Roebuck catalog, then buy a lot near beautiful Garfield Park. He paged through the furnishings available for his luxurious bachelor pad. Too much fringe for his taste, including the discreet ladies with their upswept hairdos and bustles. How much of that was real, he wondered.

Could figures really change that much? The young women of the day were upholstered very much like the furniture in the catalog. He preferred a more streamlined look, almost androgynous by comparison. The titillation of all those clothes and all that flesh, the round sensuousness of it was lost on him. He loved the sharp planes and angles of the modern body. A sharp intake of breath and memory struck like a knife. The sharpness of Julie's collarbone and the angel wings that formed between her shoulders when she turned away from him in sleep.

His mother would never meet the woman of his dreams. Even if he were lucky enough to find her again. He would never have Tess's blessing. He clicked idly on "The Music of the Night." An excerpt played from *The Phantom* as a turn-of-the-century bordello took shape on the screen. Woman lounging in undergarments that covered more than the average modern costume, perched naughtily on the knees of gentlemen old enough to be their fathers, gentlemen wealthy enough to afford the ride.

One of those creatures drew his attention. Lean and angular with enormous eyes, she looked more like the little match girl than a lady of pleasure. He reminded himself that the exploitation of children had flowered in these hot house parlors as much as in the sweat shops and factories. Something in the angle of her shoulders made his heart ache.

He closed his eyes, only for a moment. When he awoke he was staring at his mother's screensaver. He had been asleep for so long the system had thrown him off the Internet. Downstairs the fire had gone out. He stretched out on the couch, just as he would have had she still been alive, and pulled the afghan over his shoulders.

He had spent the whole night at the Virtual 1900 site when he should have been checking Tess's e-mail, looking for clues to the identity of her technical advisor. She had not been alone on the night that she died, he was sure of it. He rolled over, careful to take the afghan with him. Now that the fire had gone out, the room was chilly.

The past was a powerful magnet. Everyone was charmed by old pictures, everyone assumed that he was riding the crest of the wave, that history existed only to yield the present moment with ourselves at the center. That the past might be the focus of time and ourselves the footnote never occurred to anyone. The undisputable hegemony of the present! We were alive while these others were dead, had been folded back into time. They had lived only that they might give way to us, died so that we would be born in their place.

He was the reason now for his mother's existence, as the nineteenth had been for the twentieth century, and the twentieth would be for the twenty-first. But we were all tempted to stop time at the moment of our greatest glory and to idealize these good old days.

Half asleep and half awake, he saw Tess floating over him, saw her reaching down to pull him up so that they could float together like figures in a Chagall painting. He wanted to float away, wanted to join his mother in the ether but something held him back, something he had seen tonight and could not quite understand.

Julie! He opened his eyes in surprise, as the thought registered. The girl in the bordello, sitting on the old man's knee, the child woman who managed to look both lascivious and fearful, that was Julie. Not her face perhaps but her body, the angle of her shoulders, the way that she sat, half turned away from the old man's fondling, that was Julie!

Releasing the thought had made him weightless. He was free now to rise above the bed, to join the figure floating in the air, who changed before his very eyes from Tess to Julie and back to Tess again.

ELEVEN

It snowed all night and in the morning the streets were snarled with traffic. The magic had gone out of the air and the people were tired and disagreeable. They had shopped too long, stayed out too late, spent money they didn't have because the snow reminded them of icing on a cake and the streets sparkled like the opening strains of the Sugar Plum Fairy. This morning they knew better. They were crabby and late for work and had just realized how many months it would be before the snow finally melted in their driveways.

The streets in Tess's part of the city were too narrow to accommodate two way traffic and parked cars. The snow plows were the last straw. Drivers were stalling out while edging their way around stranded cars. Horns were beeping. Most people were content to roll down their windows and yell out obscenities but occasionally doors were thrown open and someone leapt out ready for battle.

Only the children were happy, trudging the snow mountains or throwing themselves down to make angels. Christian watched them from the window while he ate his cereal. They were still there when he pulled the front door shut and jiggled the key in the lock. This door had been hard to lock for as long as he could remember. Some special sleight of hand was required that Tess claimed was easy once you got used to it.

The newspaper was lying in its plastic bag at the foot of the steps, covered with snow. He must remember to stop delivery and he should ask Joszepa to clean out the refrigerator. His mother's house—his house now—would have to be sold and all her things disposed of. He had no other family. When this place was gone, so was his childhood.

He was late getting into work but not as late as Slater. He passed by the empty desk on his way to the lab. At first he assumed that Slater had stepped away for a few minutes. Even the centurion who beat time on the galley must have needed to take a piss occasionally. But something about the atmosphere made him linger. The programmers were chatting among themselves like schoolchildren left too long on their own. The room was growing noisier by the minute.

He looked down at Julie's replacement, now dancing in the aisle next to his desk. Two boys were tossing an imaginary football. The one in the front of the room was so involved in receiving a pass that he bumped right into

Christian. "Burton, where's Mr. Slater?" Burton's eyes grew big and he began to stammer something. That was the trouble with treating your staff like children. They lived up to your expectations.

Christian stopped a purposeful-looking girl carrying a folder, one of Julie's friends, the one who had smiled at him the day that he was assigned to the lab. "Sarah," he tried to look severe but her smile was so welcoming that he had to break eye contact. He found himself looking down while he spoke to her. "Sarah, do you know where Mr. Slater is?"

"No one knows. He's not here and he hasn't called in."

"Will you do me a favor?"

She edged closer. She smelled vaguely of cucumber and something else, mint perhaps. It must be one of those new shampoos. "When he comes in, tell him—no, just call me. Can you do that? I'll be in the lab."

"Of course. I'll call you as soon as he comes in, Christian." She hesitated slightly as though his name were a secret between them.

"Thanks," he broke eye contact and hurried away. By the time he reached the lab he was breathless. He called Human Resources but no one knew Slater's whereabouts. "Can you try to reach him at home?"

"Sure, but it's only 10:30. He's probably just held up in traffic." He could hear pages rattling as though the woman at the other end of the phone were trying to do something else while she talked to him.

"Please, this is important." He heard her sigh and there were more paper noises. "And it might be a good idea to let his staff know where he is. They seem a little restless. Oh . . . and call me back, I need to know as soon as you reach him, where he is and how soon he'll be in."

"Yes, *sir*." He could hear her putting the papers away.

Christian began to pace as soon as he hung up the phone, treading a path from his desk to the coffee station and back again. For Slater to run now made no sense. He would do better to stay and face it, to stall and delay, to wear Christian out. Meanwhile, he could make his plans, cover his tracks, so that when he finally made the break, it would be sharp and clean. Christian was a long way from knowing the purpose of the virus, what it was doing inside the files. Until he did, Slater was safe. Without a purpose, there could be no motive and no trail. What Christian had found so far could be an act of random sabotage or a corruption that had made its way into the Group through one of the clients' files.

Christian decided to make a pot of coffee. Measuring the grounds into the paper filter, filling the pot with water and pouring it into the well, these routine tasks were comforting and cleared his head. All right, he thought, when he had heard the whoosh of steam and was waiting for the coffee to drip. Let's say that he hasn't run. Let's say he's off somewhere getting ready and that he'll show up later this afternoon, cheerful and boyish, claiming not to know what all the fuss is about. If he has any brains, he'll do this as long as he can.

The coffee was ready. He rinsed out his cup, rubbing at the ring of stain first with his finger nail and then with a paper towel. Meanwhile a plan was forming in his head, a way of forcing Slater's hand and driving him into the open. It was daring, perhaps even foolhardy, but it had to be done and Christian was the only one who could do it. "Never be afraid to be the best," Gartner had told him that day in the museum. "Son," he had called him. His first day in the lab Gartner had called him son.

The slight tapping startled him. He looked up to see Sarah's face in the reflecting glass. She was standing on her toes, her hand shading her eyes, straining to see if he was in. They all did that. They knew that they couldn't see in, but they continued to peer and squint as if they could, forgetting how foolish they looked to someone on the other side of the glass.

He pressed the buzzer. "So this is where they're hiding you these days." She smiled as she slid inside. "Just wanted you to know that he's here. He just came in, looking windblown and apologetic, says he overslept. That's probably true," she winked. "He sure looks like he slept over someplace."

Her message delivered she felt entitled to do a little exploring. She was examining the workstations, glancing curiously at the report that lay on the printer.

"Thanks, Sarah," he rose from his chair, "but you didn't have to come all the way down here. A phone call would have been fine."

"That's all right," she said, as he led her to the door. "I was curious about this place. This is where you do all your tests?" She turned suddenly so that she was facing him, then reached up and adjusted his lab coat. "The collar's turned in," she ran her hands down his lapels. He could feel himself blushing. "You wear this coat all the time in here, even when you're alone?"

"It saves my clothes," he heard himself say in a high unnatural voice. He was going to explain about the air conditioning and how it was sometimes very cold, but by that time they had reached the door. "Thank you for coming," he said reaching across her to open the door.

"Not at all. If you ever need help, give me a call. I'd be *very* interested."

He looked up to see Slater standing just a few feet away, grinning at them both. "Sarah, I left something on your desk, that is, if you're finished here."

"Of course, Mr. Slater," she touched Christian's arm lightly, then she was gone.

"Your new friend?" Slater followed him inside. "I hear she's a handful."

"Sarah is interested in a position here in the lab," Christian's face had turned very red and his fists were clenching and unclenching at his sides.

Slater raised his hands. "Peace," he said, "No offense. It's just that I'm amazed at how you quiet ones always—" He grabbed Christian's arm before he could connect with his face. "Please don't do that. I already told you—"

"And I already told you that you're full of shit."

"Okay, fine, I'm full of shit. Just thought you might like to know that you've become very popular with the female members of my staff."

Christian stared. He couldn't help himself.

"Really," Slater nodded. "It's probably the lab coat. You know how women love a uniform."

Christian consulted his watch. It was almost 11:30. "You were a long time getting here this morning."

"Yes, I was."

"Some of us were worried that you weren't coming at all."

"I can tell you who has your name in the Christmas gift exchange."

"Don't change the subject. Where were you, today of all days?"

"She didn't draw your name but she traded with one of her friends. I hear you're worth big bucks."

"You sent me home early yesterday so I could get some "rest" and today you weren't here when I arrived." Christian had forgotten his plan to string Slater along, to give him just the rope that he needed to hang himself. He could feel his temperature rising. "What's going on?"

"Blond, blue eyes, comes up to about here." Slater measured the middle of his chest with his hand. "This could go very well for you."

Christian stood his ground. "I mean it. Where were you?"

"I started off for work this morning the way I always do. Then I started to think about everything we'd be facing, the two of us from this day, and when I got to my exit, I kept going. I drove to Fullerton Beach."

"This isn't exactly what I'd call a beach day."

"I sat in the car for a while and then I got out and walked. I needed to clear my head. I walked until my ears started to sting and my face got numb." Slater picked up a paper clip and began turning it over between his fingers. "Then I got back in my car and drove over here."

"What made you come back?" Christian held his breath. "Is there something that you want to tell me?"

"I was scared."

Christian waited.

"What's that disease where you're paralyzed from being in the wind too long?"

"Bell's palsy."

"That's it! Bell's palsy. My face is still numb. It feels like rubber."

"You're not going to tell me why you came back?"

"I'm here. That should be enough. Whatever you have to tell me, I'm ready to deal with it."

Christian took a deep breath, hoping that Slater would say more but he continued to avoid his eyes. "All right then," he sighed. "Let's me tell you what I found." Christian walked him through the setup of the lab. How each of the 17 workstations was set up to mimic conditions in a particular time zone, then all of them networked together to simulate a worldwide company.

"This company participates in some way in the essential industry of each time zone. There's no company like this. It's all hypothetical. They import rubber from Caracas, monitor the rain forest, run an observatory in the desert. They keep most of their money in Manhattan, but they have special accounts in Zurich and the Cayman Islands. They're always transferring money back and forth." He kept waiting for Slater to interrupt him, to tell him that he knew all this, but he just kept listening and nodding his head.

"I discovered the problem in Caracas, but it could have been anywhere. I moved the date up and then I tried to run the payroll—"

"You moved the date up? What does that mean? Dates don't go 'up.'"

Christian sighed. "I advanced from 1999 to the same month and date in the year 2000."

"Just like that? How?"

"How do you think? I used the Date/Time option on the control panel. Anybody could do it." Christian showed him.

Slater had taken a seat at the console. He was selecting time zones, watching the beam of light travel around the globe, illuminating each section in turn like the eye of God. "Hey, this looks just like the demo."

"Yeah well, you know, great minds—"

"Let me get this straight." His hair looked wispy and fly-away. He must have been so distracted this morning that he forgot the mousse. "You set the date forward to the year 2000 and nothing happened?"

"What do you mean?"

"The system didn't crash?"

"Why should it crash?"

Slater shrugged. "If I were planting a virus—out of spite, you know, or because I hated Gartner's guts," his eyes narrowed and for a minute the big man looked sincere. "I'd set it so that everything blew up on December 31."

"Would you?"

Slater nodded. "Sure."

"That doesn't take much imagination."

He chuckled. "I don't have much imagination. That's why I work here. I'm a disgruntled employee."

"That's your theory then, that the virus is an act of sabotage?"

"Isn't that what most viruses are? Pranks that get out of hand?"

"Not at all. A virus is merely a string of code that replicates itself, attaches itself to a program, performs some secret operation, then jumps around so it can't be found. It uses the power of the system against itself, just like a virus in a human body."

"So it's not necessarily destructive?"

"Oh no! A virus that destroys its host puts itself out of business. A successful virus could attach itself to the host system and operate for years without anyone knowing it was there."

"Like a spy." Slater said the words quietly as though he were speaking to himself.

"Exactly like a spy."

"And that—" he stopped to clear his throat— "that's what you think we have here? A program that spies on our records?"

"Not our records. We're only a consulting firm."

"Whose then?"

Christian made his face a mask. "Whose do you think?"

Slater broke eye contact. He ran his fingers through his hair and began to pace. Christian tensed, measuring the distance between himself and the telephone. They were in a soundproof room. That gave him only two options. The door or the phone. His eyes moved involuntarily from one to the other and back again. The door or the phone. That's all there was.

"So when we install our software, what we're really doing is planting a virus, like a mole, that burrows deep into our client's internal records. Maybe we sell them a maintenance plan so that it's easy for us to go back and siphon off information."

"Or maybe we just monitor them electronically from a remote site so that we're nowhere near the scene of the crime."

"Like tapping a phone line."

"Exactly."

"How did you figure it out?" Slater was very still. Like an animal in the second before it pounces.

Christian edged a fraction closer to the door. His lips were dry. He had to run his tongue around them before he could speak. "I can't exactly say that I've figured it out. Not really. It's just a theory that I have."

"Just a theory." Slater echoed nodding his head.

"What I do know—" Christian's voice cracked like a teenager's and he had to start again. "I know that the system is doing something with the files, writing to them, maybe, or copying them, and it has to put them back before it can respond to our commands. That's the reason for the hesitation I experienced when I tried to run the Venezuelan payroll. I saw it in the date but it could have been anywhere. The system is busy behind the scenes so that any command I give it is going to be delayed."

"What's the system doing?" Slater spoke slowly and deliberately. He had given up playing dumb.

"I have no idea."

"Then how are you going to stop it?"

"I'm not."

Slater's mouth made a big O of disbelief.

"There isn't time. I'm going to work by inference and try instead to circumvent the results."

"What does that mean?"

"There's a thief in the warehouse. I could send teams of men inside to look for him. That's the labor intensive solution. Or I could simply block the exits."

Slater stroked his chin. "And that's working by inference?"

Christian nodded. "I don't care if he gets in, as long as he can't get out."

"But what if he has no intention of getting out. What if he's a terrorist? His goal is to get inside the warehouse and blow it up."

"There's only so much I can do."

Slater sat for a long time, drumming his fingers on the arms of his chair. Christian noticed idly that he had a manicure. Christian's own nails were broken and split from pounding the keyboard, the skin ragged with hangnails.

Finally Slater spoke. He gave a deep sigh and pushed his chair back as he rose. "I want to show you something. May I?" Christian made room for him at the terminal and waited while he signed on to the Internet. "You ever see this?"

"Our website? Sure."

"See the list of international locations?"

"Yes." Christian glanced at his watch.

"They're not there."

"What do you mean they're not there?"

"All those international numbers are ringing into an empty room in the basement of this building."

"How do you know?"

"I saw one of the telephone bills. Then I went exploring one night on my own. Those international calls are relayed back here and answered by a machine."

"A machine? Like 'Hi, this is the Doomsday Group. Sorry we can't take your call.'"

"A very sophisticated machine that can mimic the human voice. I can see you don't believe me." Slater pulled a wafer thin phone from his breast pocket. "Here, dial one."

"Oh no, not the phone trick. Not again."

"Why are you so prepared to think that everything I do is a trick? While at the same time you believe that I'm too stupid to find my own dick."

Christian laughed in spite of himself. "Why are you stalling?"

"Why do you care? Why don't you just contact Mr. Gartner yourself and tell him everything that you know. What do you need me for?"

"Because there isn't time."

"Phone's right here."

"You know what I mean. To run the tests that I need, even to circumvent the program. This was the only thing I could think of."

"Confront me with the evidence, you mean?"

Christian nodded.

"Even though you have no evidence."

Christian nodded again but his gaze wavered.

"Bluff it out? Tough it out? Force me into a confession?"

Christian didn't bother to nod. His eyes were glued to the floor. He couldn't see Slater but he could hear him laughing with no sound, just a series of rapid exhalations, like a burst from a machine gun. His shoulders were probably shaking.

"You watch too much television," he said when he finally caught his breath.

"It was the only thing that I could think of." Christian spoke with what he hoped was quiet dignity.

"You know, you think I'm stupid—don't even bother, I know you do—but even I'm not dumb enough to get myself locked in a soundproof room with a crook who's twice as big as I am."

Christian telegraphed his contempt. He might be twice as big but he'd gone down fast enough when Christian caught him by surprise. That's what he was counting on this time, too—the surprise—that and the fact that he was so stupid, a big stupid *animal*— !

"Well, you've got spirit. I'll say that for you." Slater wiped his eyes. "And the real reason I'm laughing is relief. You see, when I came in here this morning, I thought *you* were the crook."

Christian's head snapped around. What kind of ploy was this? "Don't be ridiculous."

"Oh, I get it!" Slater was chuckling again. "I think you're a crook and I'm ridiculous, but you think I am and that makes you a frigging Sherlock Holmes."

"I didn't think you were a *crook*," Christian

squeaked with contempt. "I thought you were a very sophisticated computer criminal."

"Well, I thought you were a crook or the son of a crook. Either way I figured I was walking into a trap."

Christian's pulse began to hammer. "Why the son of a crook?"

"Stands to reason. You're head and shoulders above the other programmers—"

Christian could feel himself begin to blush.

"Even I could see that. And you never talk to anybody. And one day they tell me to put you in your own lab and make sure you have whatever you want. What would you think?"

"I was using the same reasoning in reverse. I figured that no one could be as dumb as you were and work in a place like this. I decided that it must be an act."

"And now?"

Christian swallowed hard.

"Don't ever try to play poker. Okay, so I'm a crook and you're the boy genius who's going to blow the whistle on me."

"I was hoping you might turn yourself in. Once you knew that you couldn't get away with it."

"Aren't I more likely to kill myself? You know, death rather than dishonor. Didn't I see a movie like that?"

"Only murderers kills themselves or traitors, people who are guilty of capital crimes."

"I see you're a reader."

"White collar crime is a big business. You'd do a couple of years in a minimum security prison, just enough time to write your memoirs. When you came out, you'd be a hero, a kind of Robin Hood who pitted himself against the system and won. And those that didn't like you, the businessmen, would hire you as a consultant."

"You're making this sound awfully good. I'm almost sorry I'm not guilty."

"I'm the one who's sorry. You leave me no choice."

Slater squared his shoulders and sighed. "I hope this doesn't involve punching."

"I'm going to have to go to Mr. Gartner. The whole thing will blow wide open. The firm will get a lot of bad publicity and you will go to jail."

Slater's face changed.

"Unless, of course, you decide to kill me. Then you'll escape now but the game will be over and you'll spend the rest of your life running."

"I'd be no good at that. That's what I decided this morning on Fullerton Beach. That's why I came back, prepared to face the music, whatever that might involve."

"I'm sorry."

"I'm the one who's sorry. Because I can't stop you by any means except force. And, no, I'm not prepared to kill you. You'll do a good enough job of that all by yourself."

"Are you denying that you deliberately stalled when I came to you with news about this virus?"

"No, I can't deny that."

"And it wasn't because you didn't believe me."

"No, everything you said is perfectly plausible. I'd come to pretty much the same conclusion myself."

"And yet you claim to be innocent."

"As innocent as you are."

"Then why did you stall?"

"Because I don't think it's a good idea to go running with news about a virus to the person who probably planted it."

"Mr. Gartner?"

"None other."

"I can't believe that."

Slater shrugged. "I didn't think you would. But I have to try and stop you. Before you get us both killed."

His fist came out of nowhere. Christian felt the impact and saw a brief explosion of light, then nothing.

TWELVE

*Z*ebulon and Boris began their correspondence in the sixth
decade of the Old Time when the East and the West were
locked in a deadly stalemate. Zebulon had seen pictures of the
tall ascetic-looking diplomat dipping his head to enter a taxi cab
outside the United Nations or arriving at the embassy with his
wife—a former school teacher—on his arm on the way to an offi-
cial banquet or reception. The sight of the tall man with the
tightly crimped gray hair and the network of lines and shadows
under his eyes always made him pause. This is the man, he
thought, a tremor of recognition running through him and stopping him as he bent over his wife's chair to kiss her cheek while
the New York Times lay open on her lap or examined a headline
over the shoulder of a passenger on the subway. They bowed to
each other occasionally at the opera or ballet. Artistic functions
were then considered safe for the diplomatic corps of both great
nations.

But the two had never spoken until the day that their secret service men clashed outside the mens room at the Metropol-
itan Museum, both having been sent to inspect and clear the area
for their respective chiefs and neither willing to give ground.
"Excuse me but his excellency General Boris Alexey will be
using these facilities," hissed the short dark Russian whose skin
had a yellowish cast and whose accent came from the vaudeville
stage. The Virginian said nothing only blocked the doorway with
his arm while he spoke into a walkie talkie. Behind him two men
in suits were moving from stall to stall, pushing up the seats and
examining under the rims of the bowls and in the flush boxes for
hidden microphones or explosives.

"Perhaps we might share the facilities," Zebulon suggested, appearing from nowhere or so it seemed to the exhausted
Virginian whose job it was to track all his movments, "Now that
you have ascertained that the area is safe." He nodded to the
agent at the door, whose name he had never bothered to learn,
then bowed to the shadows at the other side of the hall where
General Alexey himself stood waiting for the outcome of the con-
test.

"You are as anxious as I am, I think, for peace." Zebulon
spoke again as they stood side by side at the urinals. Boris made
no answer but something in his silence seemed to acquiesce or at
least to indicate that he was listening.

"I have something that I wish to give you," Zebulon said
from the sink while the warm water ran over his fingers. Outside
the door the Russian and American agents stood facing each
other in uneasy silence, broken only by the occasional squawks
from the Virginian's radio. He spoke very softly into the receiver
never breaking eye contact with his Russian counterpart. Boris
nodded and bent over the sink next to his. "I will be glad to re-

ceive it," he said in his deep baritone. After they had wiped their hands on the roller towels, identical models on either side of the door, they shook hands. It was then that Zebulon passed him the address, a safe house in a Maryland suburb, where they would each arrive alone and on foot shortly after dusk the following Monday.

This was the beginning of the historic liaison that would have cost each man his job if not his life if it had been known by their respective governments. There is much speculation among the Scorpions about the nature of the information exchanged by these two brave men. The truth is that no one knows what they said or did in that first meeting although legend has it that Boris brought a bottle of imported vodka in a paper sack and that Zebulon had smoked salmon, caviar and red onion waiting for his guest. At any rate these are the foods served every year on May 6 when the Scorpions commemorate the historic meeting although no one is sure of the exact date.

This was the first time that they met face to face and what they said or agreed can only be imagined. After this they exchanged information by courier. Some of these messages have survived, so that we know, for example, that Zebulon gave Boris the codes for disarming the American missiles and that Boris reciprocated with the details of a new personnel bomb that the Soviets had perfected. We also know that none of this information was ever shared with any research agency to gain advantage but that it was used as intended, to prevent the outbreak of hostilities between the two countries.

"Our radar listens for echoes of life on distant planets," reads a fragment attributed to Zebulon, "but we are deaf to the voices of our brothers in the East and they to us." Boris concurred and continued to supply his brother with State secrets,

particularly those which would enable the Americans to neutral-
ize an act of Soviet aggression. Zebulon did the same until each
side had enough information to hold the other's army in check. It
was only this, they reasoned, and not a treaty or any similar and
traditional show of good will that would render violence point-
less and ultimately obsolete.

Meanwhile their governments continued to stockpile
arms, to violate treaties and transgress boundaries while Zebulon and Boris watched like parents whose children are playing at
the water's edge, not wanting to spoil the game but ready to
swoop down at a moment's notice to prevent them from going in
over their heads. Some say that it was the discovery of their secret liaison that finally toppled the Communist Party, released
the countries of the Eastern bloc and ended the cold war. But this
may be a rumor started by those who cannot believe that history
unsupported by conspiracy is capable of bringing anything to
pass. Certainly the Scorpions have over the eras acquired a respect for conspiracy which is not always justified.

Zebulon and Boris were old men, ready to retire from the
service of their countries when they began to talk of dismantling
their organizations. For it would be naive to imagine that secrets
could have been exchanged on this scale without a network of
agents. They had succeeded in their aim of curbing the militaris-
tic impulses of both nations and now they began to worry about
the ease with which they had been able to obtain and to pass secrets. What would happen when they were gone, if their organizations were to fall into unscrupulous hands, or—and this perhaps betrayed a habit of suspicion that had survived the cold
war—if one side of the conspiracy were to be dismantled and the
other to continue operating. How could an operation the size of
theirs be weeded out with assurance that the roots were not

somewhere safe in the darkness and waiting for an opportune moment to sprout again.

This was the burden of their success. Having succeeded so thoroughly at conspiracy there was no way that they could warn their fellow countrymen of how easy it had been and how vast a network had been seeded. Some days they believed that the success of their operation could be traced to man's inherent goodness, but on others they were certain that the size of their operations was proof of man's instinct for treachery. Circumstances alter facts, they were fond of saying, but not always with confidence.

Each was most afraid of the other's death and how the cards might be reshuffled. "How is Zebulon this morning?" Boris inquired in a deep phlegmy voice, as an aide helped him to swing his legs over the side of the bed.

"He has spent a quiet night," the aide assured him, "and is expected to join his wife for breakfast."

"Tell him that nothing works so well as nitroglycerin." Boris spat into a small silver bowl at the side of his bed. "Let him carry the pills with him wherever he goes and give some to his wife as well. She's the only one who can be trusted not to exchange them for something else."

Not content with Zebulon's assurances that those around him could be trusted, he had personally vetted the American general's staff with some surprising results. Nor was he sure that it was safe to trust his old friend with this information. "They get senile," Boris said, apropos of nothing, "And can't tell their friends from their enemies." He gave a deep sigh, never dreaming that the aide against whom he rested his weight had been for years in Zebulon's employ.

Both men were relieved when the first rumblings of the

Y2K crisis were heard for it gave them a reason to continue the covert operations that had by now become second nature. Think of the satellites orbiting the earth, the nuclear power plants— they were almost hysterical with relief—the agencies in the public and the private sectors that are certain to run amuck. The disruption of information services and television. Think of what happens during a black out and then multiply the effects by hundreds and thousands. Nor is there any way to predict the outcome. The silos were as likely to jam shut as they were to open and release their deadly burdens against the sky.

"It cannot be allowed to happen," they said in unison and the "it" of which they were speaking gradually came to mean the twenty-first century. "Mankind is not ready," they agreed. What hung unspoken in the air between them was that mankind would never be ready. None knew better than Zebulon and Boris how careless both governments were, how susceptible to subterfuge and manipulation.

"Think of the third world," Boris hissed, "Africa and the Subcontinent." Zebulon reached for his nitroglycerin. And so it was that the Scorpions were born. They began by assessing the extent of Y2K preparedness around the globe and trying to predict the consequences. Defense and weapon systems were their primary concerns, given their backgrounds, and it was relatively easy for them to assemble the data, dismal as it was, about the chaos that could be expected, particularly in the third world, when the Millennium turned.

"All of the best scientists have immigrated to the United States," Zebulon reported, "and to the various capitals of the Soviet Union," he added hastily, "where the living standard is highest. They have left behind those least capable of grasping let alone remedying the problem in their respective homelands."

"Those countries least able to manage technology are also most eager to get their hands on it, as though it were a charm that would empower them against their neighbors." Boris shook his head. *It was clear that the twentieth century had unleashed a monster that it was not prepared to control. Their gloom deepened when they realized that the Millennium, severe as it might be, was only the first of the crises that would be unleashed. The list grew longer every day.*

"In approximately thirty years we will run out of time," a physicist told them.

"Ah, yes," Boris began, but the man would not let him continue.

"I am not speaking metaphorically, sir. We will literally run out of time. Our computers lack the capacity to go beyond the number of seconds that will have accumulated since the seventies."

"The number of seconds—?" countered Zebulon. *"Surely you don't mean that computers count time second by second?"*

"And convert it to the time that displays on screen," he nodded solemnly.

"Why does no one do anything about this?" Zebulon exploded. *"Will they wait until it becomes a crisis of the same magnitude as the two-digit year?"*

The physicist shrugged. "Each man hopes that someone else will do it. Or that some unknown solution will evolve in the interim, one that is easier or less costly. The original decision to count time was not made lightly, I can assure you. It really is the most efficient way to do it when you consider how easily and quickly the computer can add and how much longer it takes to perform other operations."

"*The mindless way is never the best way. It assumes an infinity of resources.*"

"*We had an infinity of resources.*" The physicist refused to back down, even though Zebulon was glaring at him and Boris, by far the more patient, was anxiously wringing his hands. "*At least we thought we did.*"

Later, sitting in their limousine with its smoky glass windows and two little flags flying, the Soviet to the right and the United States to the left, they tried to make sense of what they had learned. Their agents had reported their findings at length from all over the globe. A debriefing on this scale must surely hold a solution, a diamond sparkling somewhere in all this dross, hidden for the moment, its facets waiting to catch the light.

Boris was the first to speak. "*Mankind has put its future in the hands of machines.*" He spoke slowly as the miles slid by the tinted windows. "*We have abrogated responsibility for the quality of our lives from god to kings to the institution of government and finally to technology itself. At each step in our devolution we have imagined that we were improving our lot, that if we were not bettering our own lives, that we were making things better for our children. This habit of ignoring the present, of either mistaking it for the past or bartering it for the future is our downfall.*"

Zebulon, so quick witted and so passionate, could make no answer.

"*This short-sightedness is not new,*" Boris continued while Zebulon sat shrunken in his corner staring down at his hands. "*Eighteenth century England shipped its convicts to the new world and imagined that because they could no longer see the poor and the weak whom they had branded as criminals they were no longer responsible for them. That all men are brothers was a metaphor in the eighteenth century. Today it is reality. Technology has connected us and made us not only brothers but neighbors.*

"Time is running out. We have a global economy without yet having a global identity or a global conscience. That the coffee we drink from a styrofoam cup "for convenience" is destroying the rain forest, this is incomprehensible to us. We have never seen the rain forest. We cannot imagine ourselves capable of destruction on such a scale. We will not acknowledge our own power." He finished with a long sigh and for many miles, there was no sound inside the limousine but the labored breathing of the two old men.

"Then it is just as we have feared, my friend, we have come to the end of our road." The limousine was turning into the airport and for a moment their shoulders touched.

"Unless . . ."

Zebulon looked up, hope flickering for a moment in his eyes.

"Always in the past it has been you who are the dreamer, the idea man, and I, the sober Russian bear, who hold you back. But today, perhaps we will change places."

"What are you thinking?"

"Could not time be stopped?"

"What do you mean?"

"That great clock that is ticking so loudly, counting the seconds, can it not be stopped somehow, disconnected?"

Zebulon made no answer but already the tears were drying on his cheeks.

"The wire is cut, so." Boris made a scissors of his fingers. *"The hour glass turned, and mankind starts again."*

"One great power failure would do it—but there would be chaos and looting. Are you thinking of something as simple as hypnosis?" The word hung on the air between them.

"We must take them back in time, lull them to sleep as one does little children. Let them forget what they have done. The present will fall away as it does each night in dreams. When they awake, the world will seem different and they will accept what they see."

"But this thing, how will we do it?"

Boris shrugged as only a Russian can. All the fatalism of the East was in that one gesture. "It is enough for today that we know what must be done."

They began to plot how they might take technology away from the twentieth century, make it disappear, block it from the memory of man, so that it would have to be reinvented but better this time, more efficiently and with foresight. They had been boys at a time when science promised a world of wonders. Zebulon especially must be forgiven for becoming a boy again. He longed to relive those days when he stood in line on Saturday mornings to see the latest episode of Flash Gordon or Buck Rogers and sent away for a kit to build his own radio.

"Imagine a world plunged into darkness," he was fond of saying, speaking at banquets organized to solicit funds for the Scorpions. "Then slowly the lights come on, one by one. The telephone, the radio, the automobile, imagine how happy we will be to see them." In his mind Zebulon saw his mother speaking into the receiver and himself a little boy in a sailor suit standing beside her, sharing her excitement.

In the end it was his son who saw to the details, interviewed scientists, chaired meetings and finally pulled the switch.

Zebulon never lived to see the results. He was one of the casualties of the first manipulation, a kind of global shock treatment that erased the memory of technology and took the lives of those in a ten mile radius of the transmitters. A jagged bolt of lightning had scorched the earth where he stood, creating an effect not unlike the old Flash Gordon episodes of his childhood. Boris, who survived him by only a few years, was certain that he died happy.

Those who invested most heavily in the Scorpions were old men like Zebulon and Boris who dreamed of recreating the happy days of their childhood, when technology was little more than a toy. It was their sons who perfected the techniques, more sophisticated in each era, for manipulating time and their grandsons who voted whether the mission should continue or whether time should finally be allowed to move forward unimpeded. While they never attained the delights envisioned by the founders in their limousine, most Scorpions had the contentment that comes from doing what one knows to be right, no matter how difficult. The charge leveled against them by the RTN, that the old men dreamed over their newspapers while the young stood in the trenches, is considered mostly rhetoric and in any case, the way of the world.

Here is listed the means of manipulation in each of the 16 eras that have passed since that historic limousine ride:

1. Electric Shock

2. Time Warp

His mother had written (a la Star Trek) in parentheses, then the printed pages ended abruptly and he had to decipher her hand-written notes.

"Number 3 is *Breaking the time barrier in the same way that jets break the sound barrier.* And then there are some notes: *Breaking the time barrier involves going slower rather than faster. Maybe slowing the planet earth without causing a collision with other planets.* Okay, maybe. *Mass Hypnosis or some form of ritual—* that's number four. *Some form of parallel universe—all time exists side by side. You just need a way to get through the curtain.*" Aboriginal dream time was written in parentheses. His mother's scrawl had deteriorated, the way it did when she was thinking faster than she could write. Or when she was drinking. Had this been the last thing she did on the night she died?

"Hey, what comes next?" Slater poked his head around the back of the chair.

"Sorry, I can't make it out." Christian stretched and laid the papers next to his chair. The fire was getting low, the level of the brandy in the bottle at his side was even lower. "I thought you were asleep."

"Hell, no. I'm just getting into this. Here let me try." Slater loomed over him and Christian handed up the papers with a shrug.

"You think you can decipher my mother's handwriting better than I can?"

"You should see the things I have to decipher. Programmer's notes, expense statements, approving signatures." Slater settled himself back in the chair closest to the fire and began muttering to himself.

Christian yawned. They had come here directly from work, he and his new best friend. The man dogged his steps, giving him no time to rethink the decision he had made a few days ago shortly after his face collided with Slater's fist.

He had taken a cartoon fall, stumbling back against

the wall and sliding ever so slowly until he came to rest at Slater's feet. He must have blacked out. When he came to, his secretary was pounding on the door, rattling the knob, tapping the glass with her keys, demanding to be let in. He could see her head bobbing up and down in the reflecting glass.

She must be standing on her toes, straining to see in, worried about Slater, no doubt. The curly hair and the Dudley Do-Right chin made him very popular with the ladies. There was only one woman who loved him best. His mother? No, it was somebody else. He could feel himself sliding under again. The lights were too bright. Slater's head too big to keep in focus.

"Sit up," he was saying, "Come on, I didn't hit you that hard. Sit up."

Christian could hear the anxiety in his voice. He closed his eyes.

"Come on, please sit up."

This was fun. Why had he ever worried about self defense? He could bring the big guy to his knees just by closing his eyes.

"All right, then. I tried." Slater grabbed his legs and began dragging him across the carpet. He dumped him unceremoniously behind the Xerox machine then ran to the door. Christian could hear him talking to somebody. Did he have the energy to sit up? If he banged his foot now against the side of the machine, would someone come to help him?

He did. Concentrating all his strength in his foot, he reared back and connected with the side of the Xerox machine, just enough to produce a half-hearted thump.

But someone did come. In a few seconds Slater was back, crouched down beside him like a New Age waiter.

"Listen, I'm sorry I hit you, but I had to do it. I'm sorry I dragged you across the floor but you've got to listen to me. You've got to give me a chance to explain." Slater was breathing heavily. His clothes were rumpled and he smelled like sweat and fear. Christian smiled. Evidently he was a harder guy to beat up than he thought.

"No, don't do that. Don't go out on me again." Slater raised him to a sitting position and lifted his chin. "Here, drink this." Christian felt water dribbling down his chin. "That's better." Slater flopped him down again on his back. Christian felt like a rag doll in the hands of a particularly inept toddler. Any minute now he was going to find himself dragged up the stairs by one leg like Winnie the Pooh. "Get away from me!" He fought his way to a sitting position.

"You've got to let me show you what's going on," Slater begged. "You've got to see it for yourself."

"Twenty-four hours," Christian said with all the dignity he could muster. Then he slid back down.

"*Object theory,*" Slater had risen from his chair and was pacing back and forth in front of the fireplace as he read. "*Objects carry some memory of the time they have experienced inside them.* Let's see, that's number—" Slater counted on his fingers.

"Six," Christian shook his head, "that's number 6."

"Six, right!" Slater echoed. "She's painted herself into a corner though. No way she's going to make 16. *Location theory,*" he read on. "*Some locations are channels to an-*

other world. These would presumably be places where powerful events have happened in the past. Locations are imprinted with the most powerful event from their past." Slater read slowly but without self consciousness. "There's probably a way to get back to the Stone Age from the Grand Canyon. Far out in the ocean there is a memory of Atlantis," his voice trailed off. "That's nice," he said quietly, "She was a poet. Here's a good one: Brain waves transmitted through radio or television or through electric power or telephone lines. Or maybe the microwave. How many is that?"

"Eight," Christian told him, "That's only 8."

"Chemical," Slater continued. "Some form of drug or virus. Would the time change be a hallucination? Would you need to continue to take the drug or would the virus induce some mutation that would last indefinitely? Interesting," he shrugged and read on, "Magnetic theory—reverse the earth's orbit and time will go backwards. And she's got something here in parentheses," Slater chuckled. "Looks like Fast Forward/Reverse. You know, this would make a great movie." He paused and Christian called out, "Eleven!"

"She's doing better than I thought. Let's see: Mathematical formula. What formula states the relationship between time and physical location?" Slater looked puzzled. "I don't know, do you?"

"No formula. She's making it up."

"Oh! Here's a good one: "Photographs capture time. If the developing process is reversed, a chemical is released that contains the essence of the time in which the picture was taken. This method involves planting pictures taken in the year 1900 around the globe and then releasing some kind of chemical to reverse the developing process."

"That is good."

"*Time bomb: an explosion that fragments time rather than physical matter. This is the origin of the expression: Bomb them back to the Stone Age.*" Slater chuckled. "*Time and the river: There is no bank, there is only the river. Which river? The Ganges.*" His voice trailed off. "I don't get it. Never mind. It says 'Scratch River.' Instead, she's got: *Time stones or rocks. If they are heated, time speeds up. If they are cooled, time reverses. Rocks have a special relationship to time because their development is so slow that it cannot be seen by the human eye. They literally absorb time and can also release it.*"

"Maybe the time stones come from the river." Christian saw his mother on her first and only camping trip. He must have been nine. They were walking along a creek and his pockets were heavy with stones.

"What?"

"Never mind."

"And here's the last one: *Some people are powerful icons of their time. Time channellers. These individuals are keeping time on course without knowing it. Most of them are powerful—J.P. Morgan was a time channeler—he knew exactly the right thing to do because he had an almost perfect sense of what was about to happen. But some live very ordinary lives. Their almost prescient sense of what is about to happen is viewed by some as intuition. The most successful time channelers are women. The men tend to be misfits or geniuses. Many of them end up in hospitals.*

What appears to be an intuitive or in some cases psychic power is actually a vivid sense of time moving moment to moment. They seem to be a few beats ahead of us, actually they are on the very edge of the present. It is the rest of us who are behind.

Note: Dionne Warwick is not a time channeler. Andrew Carnegie may have been. But his sad eyes betray a sentimental nature, a memory of the coal fields and a sense of guilt at having abandoned his own kind—" Slater broke off.

"What?"

"I'm trying to remember what Andrew Carnegie looks like."

"There's a big picture of him at the museum, J.P. Morgan, too."

Slater nodded. He read very slowly, as though his finger were moving from word to word, as though he were sounding things out in his head. He had probably been a member of the slow reading group but it didn't seem to bother him. He was slow and thoughtful, ponderous, like a bear who lumbered, sniffing and squinting from idea to idea.

As he watched him struggling with his mother's words, Christian smiled. He was glad things had worked out the way they had, glad—although he wouldn't have admitted it—for the company.

"J.P. Morgan with his bulbous nose and swollen irascible face is the picture of corruption, entirely self-absorbed, snarling at the world as though it had somehow exploited him. He used his gifts to gain power but there was no pleasure in him."

"She must have seen those pictures. She must have been to the museum."

Slater cocked his head, at a loss to know why that should be so important.

"The day she died. I was supposed to meet her there. She said she hadn't seen it."

"When did you make the date?"

"Three or four days before. Thursday night, I think. I was watching the Bulls when she called. I didn't want to talk. I blew her off."

"Was that the last time—?"

"No, I called her two days later in a panic about something. She talked me down, invited me over for lunch. And I blew her off again. Actually, that's when we made the date. She hadn't seen the exhibit then. She would have said something."

"Maybe she *said* she hadn't seen the exhibit because she wanted you to go with her, but actually . . ." There was no need for him to finish the sentence. They both had mothers.

Christian was stung by an absurd desire to cry. He could feel the lump rising in his throat, the tears stinging his eyes. He should have loved her better. He meant to love her better but there hadn't been time. "It's all right. It doesn't matter." He swallowed hard.

Slater jumped in like an good emcee who knew how to keep the program moving. "Let's see, we've got electric shock, time warp, time barrier, mass hyposis, parallel universe, object theory, location theory, brain waves, chemical or drug imbalance, magnetic theory, mathematical formula, photography, time bomb, the river—scratch the river, time stones, and time channelers. That's—"

"Fifteen," Christian blew his nose. He was good with numbers. Other people saw images when they talked or listened. He saw numbers. "She's one short."

"Nah! She missed the easiest one of all. You could have told it to her. Even I could have told her. A virus."

"What?"

"A computer virus that sabotages all the Y2K programming."

"How would that send us back in time?"

"The computers will think it's 1900 instead of 2000."

"There weren't any computers in 1900."

"Precisely. So they'll destroy themselves. Computers are sticklers for detail. They won't let you get away with anything."

"So they destroy themselves, that doesn't make it 1900. It'll be 2000 with a lot of broken computers. It might set us back for a while, but we'd just fix them and keep going."

"It's not just the computers themselves that would break. Everything using digital electronic technology, everything with a chip in it. You know, that's a better way to transmit the virus. Put it in memory. Yes! The computers don't just blow up, they disappear and they take with them the memory of technology. Maybe there's a few computers left lying around. What's the difference? People use them for planters. Their memory of technology has been erased. This is perfect. Computers are tidy, they like to clean up after themselves. They get very nervous when their storage space is disorganized. You know, they keep sending you those lost cluster messages. Computers are actually very neurotic and they're experts on memory. That's the way to do it. Put the virus in the chip and give it instructions to destroy itself as well as its host. Vaporize, like in a science fiction movie."

"But we'd still be dressed in late twentieth century

clothes, living in late twentieth century buildings, just the way we are now, only without computers."

"But we wouldn't know they were late twentieth century clothes, would we? We'd think these were late nineteenth century clothes because that's the time we'd think we were living in. Duh?! Think about it."

Christian tried.

"You know the trouble with you is you're too much like a computer. You probably have a chip instead of a brain, so you'd vaporize right along with the technology."

"Do you mind? You're giving me a headache."

"Excuse me, but I think it's the brandy that's giving you the headache. Come on, dude. This is a story, go with the flow."

"There are too many loose ends."

"What? Tell me one."

"Calendars, appointment books, check books, everything that has the date written on it."

"Maybe. But there are a lot of Scorpions waiting in the wings. They're expecting all this confusion. Remember? While the rest of us are wandering in a daze, they're ready to step right in and get everything cleaned up. Maybe they even get us some authentic nineteenth century clothes. They probably have them stockpiled in a big warehouse somewhere."

"No rayon, no nylon, no synthetics."

"Yeah but plenty of cotton and linen and good wool. Notice how those fabrics have all come back. It's not like the 60's and 70's when everybody's wardrobe was filled with polyester. That stuff would be hard to get rid of. It's practically indestructible. But the clothes aren't important. Late nineteenth, early twentieth century clothes are whatever somebody tells you they are. You know why you think your great grandmother wore a bustle and put her hair up?"

"Because somebody showed me a picture."

"Well, some Scorpion's going to show you a picture of your great grandma in polyester and tell you it was 1860 and you're going to believe that. Why wouldn't you? It's not like they haven't done this before, you know. This is the sixteenth manipulation. They've got all the props, all the sound and light cues. It's not like the first time when poor Zebulon got himself fried like the Emperor Ming."

"Some things are bound to slip through the crack."

Slater shrugged. "Little disconnects. *Déjà vu.* Happens all the time."

"Like the feeling I get at work that I've done all this before or that somebody has. Little pieces of code that shouldn't be there. Like erasure marks. Like I was following somebody's tracks."

Slater frowned. "What are you talking about?"

"What you said, the virus. The Doomsday Virus."

"I was only talking. This is just a story."

"Is it?"

THIRTEEN

"You think your mother was murdered because she stumbled on an international conspiracy to hold back the Millennium?"

"No," Christian blinked like a man waking up from a dream. "I think she was home alone on a Saturday night, when I should have been here. I think she got so lonely and so drunk that she fell down the stairs and broke her neck."

"Whoa—wait a minute—"

"And you know what else I think . . . ?" Christian could see Julie climbing on top of him. He felt her hair graze his chest. "Tell me about your mother's theory," she said, rolling from side to side, making him dance inside her. "Tell me," she moaned, "tell me."

Christian put a hand over his eyes. "I think I drink too much. I think sometimes everyone drinks too much

and does or says things—" Sobs were shaking him so hard
that he couldn't stand. He collapsed against Slater's chest
and the big man held him, patting his back and rocking
him like a baby. "God help us," he said when he finally
caught his breath. "God help us all."

Afterwards, when he had drunk some water and
blown his nose, he was overcome by an incredible tired-
ness. Slater had retreated to the far end of the couch, as far
away as possible. "You going to be all right by yourself
here tonight?"

Christian nodded.

"I could bunk down right here. I'm so tired I could
sleep anywhere."

The space between them yawned as dark and vast
as a canyon. Christian felt a chill, a draft of dank air drift-
ing up from the abyss. "I sleep on the couch. You'd have
to sleep upstairs in—her room."

"I could do that, Christian. I don't mind."

"I do."

A cloud passed over Slater's face.

"I'm sorry. What I mean is that I'll be fine here by
myself. In fact, I'd prefer it. No, really. I'll be fine."

"In that case," Slater stood up, "I'll see you tomorrow."

"Tomorrow." Christian walked him to the door.

"I guess this lets me off the hook, huh?" he turned
back just as Christian put his hand on the knob, ready to
swing the door shut.

"What do you mean?" Christian shivered again. It
was cold in the hallway. He had forgotten his shoes.

"You trust me now, right? I can't be the one who

planted the virus." Slater's crooked grin was boyish and
charming. Guaranteed to defuse any situation. No doubt
he had learned it in business school.

"I don't know." Christian caught his eyes and held
them. "Aren't you a lady killer?"

Slater drew his breath in sharply as though he had
been struck. Then he started to laugh. "Nothing like a little gallows humor right before bedtime."

Christian smiled back. "See you tomorrow." Then
he closed the door and leaned his forehead against it.
Slater was still standing on the porch. He hadn't moved.
Christian could hear him breathing through the door. Or
maybe it was his own breathing that he heard. What did
he really know about Slater?

After all those years of sitting in the corner of the
couch frowning at Tess's dates, there was one thing he did
know. She would have loved the big man with the navy
blue eyes and the prominent chin. Chest hair sprouted
through the neck of Slater's sport shirt. They would have
argued about him, calling him a big doggie. Christian
would have meant a clumsy mouth breather who knocked
things over with his tail and his mother would have
meant—whatever women mean when they see something
that they want.

He heard footsteps receding down the steps and
into the night. He had the urge to throw the door open,
the urge shared by people who are afraid of heights, afraid
not that they will fall, but that they will hurl themselves
down. He had that same panicky impulse now, to fling
open the door, certain that Slater would be waiting like a
hungry tiger, crouched and ready to spring. Instead he

checked the locks. He put on the dead bolt and the chain, then he went upstairs.

Tess was as smart as they come. The man who lured her to her death would have to be smarter. Smart enough to play dumb or at least harmless. Then again, she was at that age when women lost their confidence, when they were prey to any man who paid attention. Why hadn't *he* paid attention? Why hadn't he—? He ran his fingers through his hair. Sleep seemed out of the question.

He climbed the stairs slowly, delaying the moment when he pushed open his mother's door and was enveloped by the smell of . . . what was it . . . peaches and vanilla? He breathed deeply, then he flicked the wall switch, remembering too late that Tess never used it. Too much light! He could have installed a dimmer for her. He turned it off then snapped on the table lamp near her bed. That was more like it. The room looked the way it always did, like a secret cave, full of scent and shadows.

He sat down on the edge of his mother's bed. Then gingerly he laid back and put his hands behind his head. So far so good. He kicked off his shoes and put his feet up. Now he could see the room the way she saw it. Every morning when she woke up, surrounded by familiar things and every night before she closed her eyes.

The door to her closet lay open, a bra suspended from the knob. He smiled. Joszepa hadn't cleaned in here after all. Those old country ladies were superstitious. He saw her making the sign of the cross, describing a narrow escape in traffic or the Communists chasing her across Europe. Tess sat beside her at the kitchen table, the two of them drinking tea. "One of these days I'm going to write your story, Joszepa." The old woman beamed. "Thanks God," that's what she used to say, then she'd make the sign of the cross.

The room was still full of Tess, full of clues to her frame of mind. What she was doing on the night she died. Who she was waiting for. His eyes panned her dressing table. Cosmetics were spilled carelessly across the top. The stool was at an angle as if she had just pushed it back and stood up. The second drawer on the right was ajar. He closed his eyes trying to remember what was inside, jewelry maybe. He should cross the room and look. He imagined a piece of paper lying somewhere in the dark, maybe in a pocket, that would tell him who had been here.

He awoke with a guilty start. The room was freezing. He looked at his watch: 4:30. My god, he had to be up in two hours. By rights he should have dreamt of Tess. She should have hovered over him while he slept in her bed and whispered her killer's name in his ear. But he hadn't dreamt of anything that he could remember. He swung his legs over the side of the bed. God it was cold! He reached down for his shoes but didn't bother to put them on.

He carried them as he padded down to his mother's office. Hard not to think of this as his room still. He could see the marks of the pennants on the walls. Why hadn't she had this room painted? He would have done it for her. Maybe she liked the pennants, a little voice whispered. Maybe she liked the memory of the time when you were here with her every day in this house. Maybe . . .

He wanted to log in to the Doomsday Group web site and visit Virtual 1900. He wanted to see the girl in the bordello, the one who reminded him of Julie. Her head was turned away from the camera but he was certain that he could recognize her. He had memorized all the angles of her face and body. Not just on the night they spent together but after, when she seemed so far away. He had sat at his desk, daydreaming, gazing at the far corner where she sat, head bent over her work.

He pressed the power switch and waited. Nothing happened. He turned it off again and then on, crawled on the floor to check the connections. When he crawled out from under the desk the screen had finally come on but it was blank. Instead of the familiar Windows log-in, the one he had set up for her, there was nothing but black, the cursor pulsing nervously in white.

All her software was gone. Her hardrive had crashed or else it had been erased since the last time he was here. He sat for a while shivering with his head in his hands.

"Do you want to go with me to the museum? They're open late tonight."

"I don't think so. Not tonight, anyway. I didn't get much sleep."

"You should have let me stay."

"Then neither one of us would have gotten any sleep. Maybe tomorrow."

"Tomorrow is Christmas Eve."

Christian blinked. It was hard to believe that Christmas was happening as usual. Lena had invited him to go with her to Midnight Mass then back to her house for a little supper. He could come early if he wanted and help her set up the tree. In fact, if he had no plans during the day, he could go with her to help pick it out. She could use some help getting it home on the bus.

"On the bus, Lena? You can't take a Christmas tree on the bus."

"Sure and why not? It's Christmas Eve."

"I'll drive you to get the tree. Why didn't you say something?"

"If you're sure it's no bother." Trust the Irish to back you into an obligation and then behave as though they were doing you a favor.

Slater was still waiting for an answer. Christian had been dodging him all day, slipping down the back stairs for coffee, taking the long way around to his lab. "What are you doing for Christmas?" he finally said.

"What I always do," Slater was staring over his shoulder. Christian wondered briefly who was passing. Mr. Gartner maybe. The image rose up in his mind but he flicked it away. "Rent a bunch of videos and get drunk."

"Don't you have any family?" He realized that he knew nothing about Slater, where he lived and with whom, who his friends were.

"No family, just me and Ebeneezer Scrooge."

Christian's eyes slid away nervously. "One of my mother's friends invited me for tomorrow night. We're going to Midnight Mass," he hedged, fighting the image of Slater alone at Christmas.

"I hate Christmas," Slater said simply, as though he could read his mind. That only added to Christian's nervousness. "What about tonight? Can you meet me?" He lowered his voice. "I have something to tell you."

"What?"

"Not here. At the museum. About 6:30. I want to see that exhibit."

Christian sighed, "All right."

Slater gave a little salute and walked away, mission accomplished. Christian stood for a minute watching him, thinking again that Tess would have liked him, that she would have invited him for dinner.

The room was dark and shadowy, the lights concentrated in the display cases. Pictures mostly and letters written by Chicago boys who had gone to war. "Fathers and Sons," the exhibit was called, "War in the Twentieth Century." It highlighted the two generations that had gone to war, traced the path of the two great conflicts, showed their turning points and where they intersected, showed the graveyards, the places where the boys were buried, the pictures of the girls who had lost first their husbands and then their sons.

Christian felt a wave of depression. He should have stopped for dinner. Eating would have made him feel better, stronger. Instead he had rushed here, eager to have the meeting over. He wanted to go back home tonight, to his own apartment in Rogers Park. He was meeting Lena for lunch tomorrow. He still hadn't picked up a gift. Maybe there was something in the Museum Shop. The whistle went off for the tour of the coal mine and he checked his watch. Slater was late.

He wandered into the next room. The Vietnam protesters colliding with the Chicago cops in Grant Park. Fathers and sons again, a middle aged cop beating a long-haired boy, doubled over in the street protecting his head while a girl in a tank top without a bra tried to pull him away. The faces of the VFW, their parade disrupted by flower children carrying posters and shouting obscenities. Mayor Daley's big jowly face looking Dickensian and larger than life as he addressed the Democratic National Convention.

Christian decided to pass on Desert Storm, men and women together in uniform for the first time and George Bush telling us to read his lips. The TV War in which the man in the street knew the names and the trajectories of various missiles and everything was "good to go." He wandered back out to the lobby. Still no sign of Slater. People were milling around, families mostly and tourists with cameras. He took a seat on the giant redwood bench near the door.

The Museum of Science and Industry was located on what had been the Chicago Worlds Fair grounds in the neighborhood near the University of Chicago. The wind stung your face as you mounted the steps, past the caryatids who stood stoically facing the lake in all weather. The museum had been founded in the thirties to celebrate the glorious marriage between industry and technology. It was the last relic of an era that believed in progress, a veritable Temple to Progress, where working men could bring their families on Sunday to celebrate the miracle of the American economy.

Many of the exhibits were sponsored by industry. International Harvester, the company that operated the steel mills where his grandfather worked, had sponsored the model farm. By the time Christian visited in the 70s, the exhibit was limited to a display of milking machines hooked up to stuffed cows with sinister-looking glass eyes. Gone was the modern farmhouse that Tess had visited as a child, the farmer himself sitting in overalls watching his new television, his wife in the kitchen canning and baking pies. Only the baby chick hatchery had survived the cut.

Christian studied the museum flyer. The exhibits seemed to have evolved, become more scientific and less industrial. He suspected that companies were no longer so eager to identify with particular technologies or processes. How Sound Travels and the Miracle of Bones and Teeth had replaced proud pictures of factory sites, chemists in industrial laboratories and the workers themselves, eyes shining, teeth flashing in gritty, sweat stained faces. The museum had become a place to bring school children, to press buttons and marvel at lighted displays, a Mecca for tourists and immigrants, but no longer the proud palace where families could celebrate the meaning of work in an industrialized nation.

Christian was glad to see that the gigantic model railroad still ran through the Great Hall, linking city and country, resources and consumers, just as it had in the days when Tess held his hand and introduced him to the wonders of her own childhood. Grandpa had been there, too, in his leisure suit, a disappointed man with a shuffling gait, embarrassed to be old, angry that the things he believed in were slipping away, suspicious that he may have been sold a bill of goods.

While they waited for Grandpa to come back from the men's room, he and Tess picked up telephones and listened to a crisis in progress. A sick child in an isolated community in the middle of the night, a light burning in a farmhouse window, the telephone wires carrying the parents' frantic call to the doctor in town and then to the pharmacy. The ambulance running out from the hospital where doctors and nurses worked through the night. And all along the outskirts, the true hero, the train that carried medical supplies when and where they were needed.

Christian looked up in time to see Slater coming through the revolving door, his face red from the wind. He held the door for an Asian family wheeling a stroller and carrying a second child. His smile came easily. The family smiled back, no longer so cold and harried and moved into the lobby, the parents chatting with animation. Christian waited a minute and then rose to meet him.

"Sorry," Slater said as soon as he had seen him. "I stopped for a sandwich, then I got caught in the Christmas traffic. Hope you weren't waiting too long."

Christian shrugged. "To tell you the truth I lost track of the time. I just sat here watching the people, remembering when my family used to come here. My grandfather worked for International Harvester. They sponsored one of the exhibits." He nodded in the direction of the model farm, forgetting that it was no longer there. "What about you?"

"I'm not from around here."

Christian let the sentence hang in the air between them, waiting but not asking for more. Then he pointed toward the Hall of the Twentieth Century and Slater took off in that direction. Christian followed, Slater's broad back was easy to keep in sight. What did it matter where he said he was from. Even if he told the truth, what difference would it make? Trust was a decision you made, not a collection of facts.

Slater was heading straight for the Century of Progress Room just as Christian had on the day that he waited for Tess. The hall they passed through was hung with blown up photographs, the faces of the twentieth century. The woman from the dust bowl, her face wrinkled and brown, the skin defining the prominent bones of her face, her hand raised in dismay or regret or simply to shield herself from curious stares. The immigrant laborer with the red handkerchief knotted around his neck, the coal miner with the lamp on his hat and the coal dust etched into the lines of his face, the black share cropper with his wild poor man's hair who looked afraid to smile, afraid of showing his teeth. And then the famous faces—Franklin D. Roosevelt and Eleanor, Harry S. Truman, General MacArthur, Babe Ruth, Louis Armstrong, even Ozzie and Harriet who had made a career out of the American family.

In between the pictures were the doors to secondary exhibits, rooms about baseball and football and music, twentieth century costumes and automobiles, dance crazes, menus of the century. Christian was drawn to each, dizzy with choices but Slater shot straight as an arrow to the Century of Progress, the special exhibit celebrating the inventor geniuses and larger-than-life financiers and industrialists whose careers spanned both centuries. Their influence reached back to the industrial revolution and forward to the turbulent sixties when the empires they had presided over—steel and finance, banking and railroads—had finally been dismantled.

Slater had stopped on the threshold. "So this is it," he said looking in awe at the interior of the blue lit room and the faces staring down at them from the walls. Slater stepped gingerly over the threshold, tripping the organ music and the neon lights running from face to face, while a voice in the darkness boomed "Welcome to the Century of Progress."

"It's like a cathedral," he said, when he recovered from the shock of it. The lights had dimmed, except for the blue still flickering expectantly around the room.

"More like an elephant graveyard," Christian countered. "Look at this," he pointed to a life size cutout of Edison, who had the wide-mouthed face of Buz Sawyer in the old comic strip. He had meant to call Slater by his first name but he couldn't remember it. It was funny, although he chose not to linger on the thought, the difference between what Slater knew about him and what he knew about Slater.

"I bet he feels left out," Slater had stopped in front of the placard listing Hieronymous Gartner and The Doomsday Group as the exhibit's major sponsors.

Christian smiled uneasily. This was where he had come upon Gartner the last time. His spine tingled with anticipation. The organ blared again as someone new entered the room. Christian jumped. Only the Asian family that Slater had spoken to at the door. They bowed shyly and moved on.

"Born too late," Slater was humming and improvising new words to the old song. "I'll never share a tycoon's fate," he crooned. "Why was I born too late?"

"Come on," he hesitated again, thinking that

Slater's name might come to him if he didn't think about it. "Let's see the rest of the exhibit."

"Relax," Slater laughed as though he could read Christian's mind. "He's not going to hear me. It's Christmas, he's out celebrating with the other millionaires. Or maybe he's already tucked in for the night, anxiously awaiting the annual appearance of his old partner Jacob Marley. Scrooge," he called out in a hoarse ghostly voice, "Scrooge."

"He's been very generous to me." Now would be a good time to ask about his mother's funeral. Who had told Slater to take good care of him? Gartner himself or someone buried deep in the executive offices, someone Christian had never heard of. "Richard," he began as the name came back to him.

Slater seemed not to hear. "This is as good a place as any to tell you what I found." He steered him to a bench against the far wall. "You know what they say about hiding in plain sight."

"I'd rather keep moving," Christian shook off Slater's arm.

"Welcome to the Century of Progress." A small boy had escaped his parents and was running in and out of the room. "Welcome—Welcome." The organ blared on and off and then on again.

Slater was chuckling as they moved on but Christian was edgy and kept watching for someone, he supposed it was Gartner, out of the corner of his eye. This was the spot where it had happened. He saw his hand reaching for the card, frozen in time, like Michelangelo's Creation.

He had made a fetish of not turning the card over. As though the telephone number were a magic charm that could only be used in times of direst need. He had carried it in his pocket for days, taking it out every night and giving it the place of honor on his dresser, then carrying it back to work with him the next morning.

That had stopped when he found the virus. Now the card sat buried in a drawer, waiting for him to decide what to do next. We've got to tell him, he wanted to say, but it was Slater who spoke first.

"Someone is selling off the assets of the Doomsday Group," he blurted as they rounded the corner and stopped in front of a replica of Edison's laboratory. The furniture and instruments had been borrowed from the Henry Ford Museum at Greenfield. "Did you hear what I said?"

Christian nodded. He could see both their faces reflected in the shatter-proof glass that sealed off the display.

"Everything is being converted to gold and stashed away in Switzerland or the Cayman Islands."

"Like we were going out of business?"

Slater nodded.

"What are you going to do?"

"Look for a job."

"I mean really."

"So do I. Maybe grab a little gold for myself since no one will be in a position to object."

"You'd actually do that, without trying to alert anyone? Just grab your share and run?"

"Who would I alert? Who can I trust? Do you

know what this says about our organization, even about the model itself?"

"That it's a replica of a real organization, doing business around the world and preparing for an international monetary crisis."

Slater closed his eyes wearily.

"There could be a very simple explanation, you know. The Y2K fixes may not work, but that doesn't mean that we engineered the catastrophe. We're just hedging so however it goes, we're not caught short."

"Suppose we've been copying our clients' records and we realize that we're about to get caught."

"Copying our clients' records is not necessarily a bad thing, especially not in the event of a worldwide crash. We could just be backing up our clients' records."

"Secretly backing up our clients' records?"

"Not secretly, just quietly, on a need to know basis, for the sake of security."

"And you don't 'need to know,' even though you're testing the system? And I don't need to know, even though I'm in charge of the programmers?"

"Maybe they don't trust you," Christian snapped without thinking.

"What's that supposed to mean?"

"Maybe they're testing the backup to see how secure the program is. Maybe they're waiting for us to come to them with the information we've found. You know they wouldn't necessarily publicize their fears about the real effects of Y2K, it wouldn't exactly be good for business."

"Christian, wake up! They're behaving like everything's about to blow up. And since they're in a position to know, I would suggest that we all follow their example and take cover."

"Cover your ass, you mean."

"That's exactly what I mean. Look at you, the boy genius, the absent minded professor, brought in to test the system when it's way too late in the game to do anything about the results, and when as far as that goes, you don't know anything about business anyway. Push the envelope, they tell you, whatever the fuck that means."

"You're the one who told me that."

"I know. Me, the world's dumbest manager of programming services. The inmates are running the asylum while the brass are working behind the scenes, converting the assets to gold bullion so when the crash comes, they're protected. Does that sound like a responsible company to you?"

"I'm not denying that what you're saying could be true. It does sound plausible in that kind of dog-eat-dog way that I'm sure you were trained to think is the way of the world. But I'm a scientist, Richard, and I was trained to never assume."

"You were *trained*," Slater mimicked, "to stick your head up your ass. Who do you think they're going to blame when everything goes wrong?"

"Not us," Christian laughed. "No one knows about us."

"I sense we are about to have our fifteen minutes of fame, maybe longer depending on how much time they need to get away."

"And who would 'they' be, Mr. Nixon?"

"Hieronymous Gartner, the man behind every

move this operation makes, and don't you think otherwise. He's a multi-tasker, a corporate genius . . . "

Christian felt a thrill of pride.

"And his staff is a bunch of fools, kids out of college, yes-men and idealists. He'd bring in The Three Stooges, if he had their phone numbers."

Christian's face stung as though he had been slapped. "I'm sorry," he said quietly, "but I don't agree with you."

"You don't agree with me! Why am I not surprised?" Slater pinched the bridge of his nose. "When am I going to learn?"

"What is it, Richard? What's wrong?"

"I was suspicious of you from the start, the way they moved you up and around, even though you had no experience, that business with the girl—"

"What business? Julie? Do you mean Julie?"

"I didn't think it through, you know." He waved his hands rhetorically, as though this was the last straw, as though he had finally had enough and was about to break off relations with himself. "I never do. I took a chance, now I'll have to pay for it."

"What are you talking about? Tell me what you know about me."

"I've already said too much." Slater began to walk faster, pushing for the exit.

"Richard," Christian called after him. The possibility that Slater might be suspicious of *him*, that he was dogging *his* steps had just dawned on him and was giving him a headache. "Richard—"

Slater turned. There was real fear in his eyes. "Just

give me a head start. Before you talk to him. A head start, that's all I ask." He stumbled backwards with his hands raised, as though he were calling for time out.

"This doesn't make any sense," Christian called after him. "We're both in the same position. We have to trust each other."

"Welcome," he could hear the voice behind him as he followed Slater down the hall, "Welcome to the Century of Progress."

FOURTEEN

Lena bought him lunch at the Greek's on the corner. He had been coming here with his mother and Lena since he was child. The place changed hands periodically but it was always a Greek who bought it—at least as far as Lena could tell. Christian suspected that this latest Greek whose pretty black eyed daughter handled the register and whose cousins bused dishes in and out of the kitchen was actually an Arab.

Lena was his mother's oldest friend. They had grown up together in the old neighborhood. Tess might network with artists and writers or sleep with attorneys because they could afford the best restaurants, but Lena remained her friend, the one she confided in, the one she relied on when there was trouble.

Unlike Tess, Lena had not aged well. Her skin was lined and puffy. A cigarette burned at her side even while she ate. She loved her martini before dinner and her friends had sense enough not to telephone after 7:30. She still dressed the way she had in high school, not a bad style actually. Her wardrobe was based almost entirely on blazers, skirts and sweaters. She wore her hair in a classic Buster Brown that she insisted on coloring herself even though Tess said she could afford better. But then Tess would have said that. Hair color was one of her values.

It could be said in Lena's defense that, although she wasn't young and attractive like his mother, although she wasn't stylish and up-to-date, and everyone flirted with Tess and ignored her when they went out together— so consistently that once in a fit of adolescent rage and probably latent sexual jealousy, Christian had accused his mother of hanging out with Lena because she made her look younger—she hadn't changed much since she lost her looks at 40, a good 15 years ago. For all her old neighborhood ways, her condition could be described as critical but stable.

That was another thing, Lena didn't just look older, she actually was older, by at least five years. "I was your mother's baby sitter," she used to say. "We started palling around together when she was only 16." Lena took her young friend shopping and to the beauty school to have her hair done until Tess was old enough to know better. When Tess went off to college downstate, the neighborhood assumed the friendship was over. They were wrong. Despite her protest marches and granny gowns, Tess went out of her way to stay in touch with Lena.

You had to admire her loyalty or question, as

Christian did, her confidence about rising in the world, her ambivalence about leaving the old neighborhood.

"Are you enjoying that, Christian?" Lena speared a french fry with her fork, dipped it daintily in ketchup and swallowed it whole.

Christian nodded between bites. "The Greek" made a great cheeseburger, even though the cole slaw was a little off, a shade too tangy, as though it had been around for a while. They substituted sweet pickles when they ran out of dill and pretended not to understand the difference, but all in all, it was a good meal in the Lena tradition.

"Make sure you save room for dessert," she said as she always did. "They've got banana cream pie." It had been years since he had craved the pie made of too-sweet pudding in a soggy crust, but Lena liked to watch him eat it while she drank her coffee. "Ah, Christian," she used to say, "I envy you your appetite."

He never had the heart to suggest that she put out her cigarette and he always averted his eyes discreetly when she had to cough. They made a good pair, the two of them, in their booth near the window, while the "Eye-tal-ian" lights twinkled overhead in the plastic pine boughs and a glittery Rudolf leapt across the cash register, with "Seasons Greetings" spelled out in plastic script over his head.

He went with Lena to the Christmas tree lot on Damen, held her selections up with one hand to see if the trunk was straight then twirled them looking for bare patches. They chose a short needled spruce. Tess preferred a Scotch pine but then Tess had Joszepa to clean up after her. Lena didn't want the trouble of all the needles and anyway, she liked the spruce better, she always had, it had a neater look to it.

Christian set it up for her in the stand, poured the sugar water into the bowl as she instructed, then placed it neatly in the center of a white bedsheet, with cotton batting wrapped around the outside. He was conscious of performing a precise ritual that Lena had learned in her early days on the south side. He suspected she had not had a tree for herself in a long time and that she was doing this for him.

The miniature stable that she placed on the bedsheet under the tree had real straw on the roof. It had belonged to her mother, she said as she set up the figures, stationing Mary and Joseph inside on their knees, but leaving the manger bare until the Baby Jesus should be born at midnight. She had only one strand of lights, and when Christian plugged them in, nothing happened. Lena was ready to test them one by one but Christian insisted on making a contribution. He ran down to the corner drugstore and bought two new sets of the Italian lights she had admired in the restaurant, one in red and one in gold. While he was there he bought the fanciest bath set he could find and some more wrapping paper. He already had a silk scarf from the Museum Shop and it was gift wrapped, but he felt that he needed something more.

Lena was just bringing down the dusty old ornament boxes from the top shelf of the closet, when he came back. She exclaimed over the lights, claiming that they were too fine and they'd show up the old ornaments. Tess usually did a theme tree, Native American or Victorian, it changed from year to year. What she did with the old stuff, Christian never knew. Lena had the ornaments she had brought with her from the south side and stringy icicles, the old kind that tarnished and tangled, draped over a piece of cardboard and held in place with a rubber band, resting inside the pages of an old Saturday Evening Post.

When the tree was up, they'd had Stouffer's macaroni and cheese on trays in front of the television while they watched *The Nutcracker*. Lena dozed off in the middle and he had to wake her at 9:30 so they could leave early enough to get seats for the Midnight Mass. This was the Christmas that Tess had grown up with, he thought, as they walked to the church in silence. She would have smiled to see him partaking of the old rituals, safe in the traditions that she had walked away from but never quite abandoned.

After Mass, which had gone on forever, featuring three priests and some very bad singing by the adult choir, they went back to Lena's and broke open the champagne. Lena exclaimed over her gifts—"Christian dear boy, you shouldn't have"—and watched anxiously while he tried on the leather gloves with the fur lining. "I wanted to get you something good, like your mother would have." Then she brought out a deli tray she had ordered especially for the occasion with side dishes of potato salad and cole slaw served on a plastic plate shaped like a Christmas tree.

He left Lena's at 3:00 just as it was beginning to snow, big soft fluffy flakes that made the streets look like the inside of a paper weight. He felt a deep sense of exhilaration as he walked along swinging his arms from side to side, as though he had passed through some ordeal and made it safe to the other side.

"Lena," he had said to her quite casually as he tore open the little foil packet of Miracle Whip and squeezed it on to his bread. "Did you know my father?"

She had been listening to Bing Crosby sing White Christmas. Her eyes were shining with champagne and good will. When she didn't answer, he thought perhaps she hadn't heard him and wondered if he should repeat the question or let it go until another time. "I'm not ignoring you, Christian," she said still with that far-away look in her eyes. "I'm just thinking about your mother and what she'd want me to say to you."

Christian speared two slices of turkey and one of ham with his little plastic fork and piled them on his bread, then he added another layer of Miracle Whip. He considered but rejected the idea of Muenster cheese, never looking at Lena, focusing all his attention on building the sandwich.

"You mustn't judge her harshly, Lamb."

"I don't," he insisted, sawing patiently with the plastic knife. "I don't judge her at all. She was a good mother to me—"

"The best!"

"But I want to know who my father is, that's all. Don't you think I have a right to know?"

"Did you never ask her?"

"I did," Christian was falling effortlessly into Lena's own speech patterns, mirroring her, courting her good will. "She said that it wasn't important. But it is. To me."

Lena sighed and took another swallow of champagne. "Christian, you know it may be true what her dad always said, that she didn't know."

"Do you mean that you don't know? There wasn't a special boy?"

"They were all special boys. She never went with a man she didn't care for. But those were strange times and she felt a need—stronger than the urge to be with those boys—to prove that she was free. Not like her mother and the others had been. Do you understand, Lamb? Can you put yourself in her place?"

He chewed thoughtfully and swallowed before he answered. "No."

"Christian, you're a good boy, an honest and a truthful boy. You can't pretend. No more than she could. If she didn't tell you it was because she didn't know."

"January 16, 1970, where would she have been and who was she with?"

"January 1970?"

"The war was going on."

"Oh God, the war! The boys were coming and going. It was a terrible time. But we were young and God help us, we enjoyed herselves."

"She was still away at school, wasn't she? You wouldn't have known her friends."

"Now wait, wait. They had those long vacations, the whole month of January. I got her a job checking out groceries at the Jewel. My brother-in-law was the manager. They made good money, those checkers. It was all Union in those days."

"Did you see her? Did you talk?"

"Of course I saw her. She lived right next door. We were out together every night on the vacations, except when she was with, you know, her other friends, the hippies and such, I didn't care for those boys with the girls' hair. How old was I now?" Lena counted on her fingers. "Oh Lord, that was the Christmas I broke up with Mike and he started dating that snooty bitch from Sabina's. Married her, he did, and she gave him nothing but grief until they split up, after four children. You should stick with your own kind, I always said. Her father was a doctor. The way she carried herself you would have thought the sun shone out of her asshole."

Christian giggled in spite of himself. "Come on, Lena, concentrate."

"I am. But God, I was so sunk in misery. I doubt I had time for anyone else."

"If I brought you her album, would you recognize the faces?"

"Lamb, I don't know. It's such a long time."

"She used to date boys from the neighborhood. Don't I look like anybody you used to know."

Lena peered at him. "A little like Ralph O'Flaherty around the eyes, God rest him." She made the sign of the cross. "He died before you were born. A sweet boy, he was and he had your gentle ways."

"Did she date any soldiers?"

"You know all the boys from the neighborhood ended up soldiers, unless they were teachers and such, and some of them had to go all the same. Of course, a soldier wouldn't have been to your mother's taste, but she would have known them all, one way or another."

"There was one picture that she kept in the bottom drawer of her desk away from the others. I always wondered if he could be the one." Christian let the sentence trail off.

"Why didn't you ask her?"

Christian shrugged, still keeping his eyes down.

"What did the boy look like?"

"Like a soldier. He was young, standing under a tree, with his shirt off."

"They were all soldiers." Lena frowned. "Can you bring me the picture?"

"It's gone now. I looked for it."

Lena picked up her sandwich with both hands and bit into it daintily.

"You're sure you can't remember any of the boys she dated in her senior year?"

She chewed thoughtfully. "You know it's very strange, but there is one that I can almost remember. He had a long foreign sounding name. She went on about him for months, then one day she clammed up and I couldn't drag another word out of her."

"Did you meet him?"

"I don't think so, although there was that good looking one that used to hang around the Jewel at all hours waiting for her. My brother-in-law had to ask him to leave. It was hard for him. He had a stutter, you know."

"Tess's boy friend?"

"No!" Lena scolded, "my brother-in-law Sandy. Something like that would have put him off. But no, that couldn't have been the one. His name was that common, Schultz or some such. It couldn't have been him."

"Was he a soldier?'

"I don't know, I tell you. Something happened between them but she would never say. Except, Jesus, I just remembered—"

"His name?"

"Not exactly, but what she used to call him." Lena stopped short, her hands steepled in front of her mouth as though the words were a secret that must be held back, "My Hero."

"Are you sure?"

"My Hero," she smiled at the memory.

The parking lot was deserted as Slater had known it would be. But he took no chances. He parked his distinctive little red Corvette on a side street three blocks away. The floor was littered with styrofoam cups that rolled and came to rest as he pulled up the parking brake. He locked the car, looking around first to see if anyone were watching. Then he walked to the office, taking a different route to throw off pursuers, even though he saw nobody.

Christmas Day. The streets were wet and dismal. The snow had melted. Some of the toys were already broken. Families who had felt tears sting their eyes as they gathered last night around the tree were by now tired of each other. But no one could leave. Not for hours and hours. *It's a Wonderful Life* was the only thing on television.

His watch said 1:30 by the time he reached the old factory on Blackhawk where the Doomsday Group had its offices. The building stood out grimly against the gray sky. Empty houses look as though they are resting, waiting for their owners to come home but empty offices have an abandoned ominous look. He pressed his security badge against the plate and the light switched from red to green. He pushed open the heavy door. Christmas music was playing softly in the lobby.

He took the stairs instead of the elevator. The pneumatic door closed with a whoosh behind him as though it were pushing him inside. The floor ahead was dark and full of shadows. The lights came on one by one as he passed the sensors. The programmers' cubicles were decorated for the holiday. Little bits of cheer caught his eye—family photographs, drawings of Christmas trees and mangers by somebody's kid, a philodendron strung with Christmas lights. He made a pot of coffee, helped himself to a peppermint from the jar on someone's desk. Then he settled down to work.

Time passed and the lights went out in the hall. He clicked his way through the files, moving line by line, reviewing the documentation for each charge, stopping occasionally to print. Gray light was fading from the windows but he didn't notice. His monitor had become the only light in the room. If his leg still cramped, he didn't notice. He no longer felt the need to stretch. Sometimes he thought he heard a sound but he kept on working. When the elevator started up it seemed very far away.

Christian dialed Slater's number and let it ring. Clarence had just gotten his wings. The whole town was in Jimmy Stewart's living room. Zuzu smiled at her father and he lifted her up. Christian decided not to leave a message. After a while he went for a walk. He thought he might stop for coffee but nothing was open. He drove to the lake instead and watched the kids trying out their new roller blades. At 3:30 he gave up and drove to the office.

It was dark by the time he arrived. The night lights were on in the lobby, the elevator door stood open. Christian stepped inside and pushed the button for the eighth floor. What kind of a guy goes to work on Christmas Day? He sighed in disgust and fumbled for his key card.

The office was dark and shadowy. No surprise. As he entered the lights came on and stayed a step or two ahead of him as he moved down the hall. In the men's room the hand dryer came on ahead of the lights and startled him.

Someone had turned out the lights in the programmers' room. You could do that if you wanted, deactivate the sensors and use the wall switches instead. Slater's screen was glowing in the darkness. Christian chuckled. Where else? He should have known. Hard at work as usual. Slater's head was resting on the desk.

He thought about creeping up on him then decided against it. "Hey, slacker!" He called out as he approached the desk. "Dude!" Still no movement. "That must have been some party." His hand was touching his shoulder when he saw the dark pool under Slater's head. Coffee? But there was no cup. He felt something sticky on his hands.

He retched in the darkness, afraid to turn the lights back on. Slater's throat had been cut. Christian had never seen so much blood. He grabbed a handful of paper and tried to wipe his face and hands. Then he stumbled off the platform and literally crawled through the maze of cubicles in the direction of the door.

If he could get back to the men's room, he could wash off his face and hands. Then he could call. Somebody. There was so much blood. What if Slater was still alive? He hadn't thought to feel for a pulse. What if the killer was still there? He huddled in the darkness, frozen with fear, unable to move. Afraid to go, afraid to stay.

FIFTEEN

The undertaker was the first person that he called. Not to take the body away. The police had already done that. He saw it on the news. Sitting at the counter of the all night diner on Hermitage with the man in the blue suit crying softly to himself in the corner.

The counter boy had stepped into the kitchen. He was probably the only one working. Christian could hear water running and the clatter of dishes.

When he looked back up, his picture was on the screen and the newscaster was describing him as an associate of the victim whose finger prints had been found at the scene of the crime. Christian sat with his coffee cup poised in midair while the newscaster gave his name and address. Then very quietly he put the cup down.

The man in the corner had covered his eyes with his hand. Water was still running in the kitchen. Christian stood up very slowly and looked around. He pulled a 5 dollar bill out of his pocket and left it under the cup. He was halfway to the door when he thought about what he had done, returned to his place, took the 5 back and put three crumpled one dollar bills in its place. He didn't want to be remembered.

There was a telephone on the corner. He hesitated, afraid of being seen. Traffic was slowly building up, people making their way home from grandma's with the kids asleep on the back seat. He had cleaned himself up as best he could in the Clark Station on Ashland. He had washed his hands and face and rinsed out his mouth but the smell of vomit still clung to him and he was pretty sure there was blood on his clothes.

He needed a change of clothes but where could he go? The police had his address. He might be able to beat them to his mother's house but it was only a matter of time before they waited for him there, too. If only he had told Gartner about the virus the first day that he found it, none of this would have happened. Poor Richard, he couldn't think of him without seeing that yawning wound under his chin.

It was too late to turn himself in. He'd have to explain why he hadn't called the police in the first place, why he had waited until his picture came on television. The police liked murder. It was their business. It might be hard to make them understand how it put other people off, literally froze them in their tracks and made them forget where they were and what they were supposed to do next.

He was approaching a newsstand. A quick glance confirmed that it was too soon for headlines. He bought a package of mints and got change for the phone. He felt in his coat pocket for the card he had put there days ago. Just touching it made him feel safe. Mr. Gartner would send a car for him, get him off the street. But first there was something he had to know.

"Thatcher Randall," the man answered on the first ring.

"Mr. Randall, is that you?"

"Yes, this is Thatcher Randall. Who is this please?"

"This is Christian Wahr—Wahrmutter," he had just remembered the television in Randall's office. "I'm surprised to find you at work on a day like this," he said as his breathing returned to normal.

"Yes, well I wish I could say that Death takes a holiday. But that's not what you called to hear about. What can I do for you, Christian."

"It's about my mother's funeral, the bills."

"Nothing to worry about, son. I thought I told you. It's been paid for."

"You did tell me. You said that a man named Slater called from the Doomsday Group."

"That's right."

"Do you remember anything else about the payment, how it was delivered, who signed the check?"

"Some of that might be in the file. Our bookkeeper usually calls to confirm large personal checks, anything not issued by an insurance company."

"This was a personal check?" Christian felt his mouth go dry.

"Oh yes, Mr. Slater delivered it himself. It was in

the afternoon, right before the start of the visitation. I remember because he asked to see the body."

"What did Mr. Slater look like, do you remember?"

"Oh yes, a very distinctive man."

"Tall, good looking man, my age, with reddish colored curly hair?"

"Oh no, Mr. Slater was a distinguished gray-haired man. About my age, I would say. He spent about half an hour with the body. I suggested that he sign the register but it must have slipped his mind."

"Are you sure?"

"One doesn't forget a man like that. He arrived in a Lincoln Town Car. His chauffeur stood outside in the parking lot, smoking, while he waited for him. Is something wrong?"

"No, it's just that—I would like to see the check. I'd like to see how it was signed, the bank that it was drawn on."

"Of course we don't still have the check, but my bookkeeper may have made a copy. She often does with a personal check that size. She'll be in tomorrow if you'd like to call back or I can ask her to call you."

"I don't suppose there's any chance that you could look for it yourself? I—I'm sorry to be so much trouble. It's just that I'm in the neighborhood and it would be so easy to drop by. I won't be around tomorrow. I have to go out of town."

"Well, I guess I could find it. If it's here, that is. Like I said, she doesn't copy every check, but a large personal check like that one, there's a good chance. Why don't you give me half an hour to check the files or better, why don't I call you when I've had a chance to take a look. Give me the number where you are."

"I can't do that. I'm calling from a pay phone, but I can stop by in an hour, when we finish dinner, my friend and I. Would that be all right?"

"Of course. I'll be working downstairs. Just ring the bell."

"Thank you, Mr. Randall. Thank you very much. And Merry Christmas."

"Merry Christmas, Christian. I'll see you in an hour."

He caught a taxi just as it was rounding the corner. Most of the traffic was going the other way and they made good time. A car was pulling out of the lot just as they pulled in. Christian thought of asking the driver to wait, then decided against it. Taking taxis made him too easy to trace. He'd do better on a bus if he could find one. Maybe he'd just call Gartner from Randall's office. He reached in his pocket and fingered the card.

There was a large wreath on the door. He studied it as he rang the bell and waited on the porch. The lights were on but the door was locked. He rang the bell again. It was cold on the porch. His breath made a mist in front of his face. He rapped a few times with his hand on the door. If Mr. Randall were downstairs, perhaps he wouldn't hear the bell. Or maybe there was another entrance around the back.

Of course, he thought, as he walked down the stairs and followed the driveway to the back of the parking lot. This is a funeral home. There has to be a back entrance. They wouldn't carry a body in through the front. Christian shivered. When Mr. Randall said he was working, what exactly did that mean?

There was a door in the back with a small lighted bell positioned discreetly beside it. He pressed it firmly. A buzzer echoed inside. He waited politely then pressed the bell a second time. Then he thought about turning the knob. The door was unlocked and swung open easily. "Mr. Randall?" He pressed the bell again as he stepped inside. The hall was dimly lit and uncarpeted. There was a stretcher standing empty on the far wall, the kind that folded up and fit easily into the back of a small van.

He shifted uneasily, unsure of what to do next. This must be where they prepared the bodies for viewing. The stretcher stood next to a door that was partly open but he didn't think it would be a good idea to go exploring. He thought about going back outside and calling. Wherever Mr. Randall was, he must be near a telephone.

He decided that he would go as far as the open door and peer around it, just to see if there was a phone on the other side. If there was, he'd use it to call the funeral home's main number and see if Mr. Randall answered. If not, he'd go look for a phone. Maybe try the front bell one more time before he left. He tried not to think about the fact that time was passing and the police were looking for him.

Mr. Randall might be sitting this minute aghast in front of his television set. He might be on the phone with the police telling them that Christian was due here any minute and offering to stall him till they got here. That's what this waiting might be about. He walked boldly across the room and pushed the door open. He had no time to waste.

It was just as he thought. He had stumbled into the room where they prepared the bodies. There was a large double sink against the wall. The wall and floor were lined with sandy colored ceramic tile and there were drains set at various points in the floor. A gurney stood near the sink, its occupant shrouded with a sheet. In the center of the room was a large steel table. Mr Randall was lying on it fully dressed with his hands crossed over his chest. From where he stood he couldn't see blood or a wound but there was a strange smell and the air seemed to vibrate.

Christian was grateful for the double sink and the drains. He heaved a few times but his stomach was empty, so he splashed his face with water and leaned his forehead for a few minutes against the cool tile. He could hear police sirens in the distance when he finally stumbled out the back door.

The police wouldn't expect him to be on the south side and he doubted that whoever placed the call had gone so far as to mention his name. That meant he was safe for a few hours if he stayed away from busy streets and places where people were likely to be watching television. The holiday was in his favor. He suspected the police were short-handed, like everyone else on Christmas Day.

What were his chances of finding a phone within the next few blocks? A bar would be no good. They'd have the television on. Maybe a gas station or a convenience store, at least until the shift changed. His watch said that it was only 8:30. This day would never end, he thought, as he began to walk. He had to remind himself not to skulk, to let go of the shadows, to hide in plain view.

There was a telephone on the next corner, just under the streetlight. He remembered when phones had been in booths with doors that closed. This one was hung on a metal pole, slung low to accommodate drivers who wanted to use the phone without leaving their car. He swore that if he survived this night, he would get himself a cell phone. He didn't care what it cost or how stupid people looked walking down the street with a phone stuck to the side of their head, cheerfully talking to someone who wasn't there, and ignoring all those who were. A cell phone, tomorrow, that was his only goal.

He got the number from information, begging the operator to read him all the Helen Carvers until he heard a number that he recognized. Something urgent in his voice convinced her to do it. "I could lose my job, you know," she said. "That's not how we're supposed to do it."

"I know and I wouldn't ask, except it's really important."

"Life and death?"

"Life and death," he echoed solemnly.

"Shit, who cares? I'm going to quit anyway. I hate it here. You're not allowed to give service. They want you to sound like a machine. Here goes. You ready?"

He took down the third number she read to him. "Thank you," he said. "Thank you so much."

"You want to hear the rest? Just in case? I'm not going to do this again."

"No, I recognize it. This is the one. I'm good with numbers."

"Oh yeah? You want mine? You got a cute voice. Are you cute?"

"No. I mean, thanks, thanks for everything, but I have to make this call. Thanks, really."

"All right, all right. You're welcome," she clicked off.

Christian hoped that wasn't one of the calls that was monitored for service.

The phone was answered on the third ring by a man who sounded like he had a cold.

"Is Helen there please?"

"Who's calling?"

"This is Christian Wahrmutter, Tess's son. Is this Ernest?"

"Oh Christian, I remember your mother." The man had begun to cry. What a nice guy. "Helen isn't here," he said. "She's gone."

"Gone?" Christian echoed. "When will she be back?"

"They just called me. An accident on the turnpike. She was coming back from her mother's. She wanted me to go with her but I couldn't—" He was sobbing so hard that Christian could barely make out the words.

"Ernest," he said, trying to calm him, "Ernest, I'm so sorry. Is she in the hospital?"

"She's gone!" he insisted. "They just called."

"What kind of accident?"

"Something about the brakes. What difference does it make? What difference does anything make?"

Christian put down the phone.

When he thought about it now, sitting in his dacha by the Black Sea, with his grandchildren playing at his feet, he regretted all the killing. It had been Zebulon who organized everything. Boris claimed that he didn't need to know the details. Now that his old friend was gone, depression had gotten the upper hand and he wondered how many he could have saved if only he had insisted on the use of other means. Torture perhaps, even hospitalization on the grounds of insanity. They had done it all the time in the old days or so his father had said.

It was bad enough in the beginning when their organization was made up of military and diplomatic operatives, people who had agreed to risk their lives in the service of their country. Occasionally someone stumbled on a file or picked up a telephone or walked in on a meeting. They were usually given the choice of joining them. It was amazing the number who said no, who were willing to give their lives for the sake of their integrity. There were others who thought they could play along. Poor fools, they were always discovered and dealt with, perhaps too harshly. Then there were those who thought the conspiracy was a good idea and were eager to join, not so many though, as you would have thought.

Each time they had to interrogate someone, Boris felt his own beliefs challenged, his own face slapped while the question was repeated over and over, himself the target who must be executed. Only military discipline had made it bearable. With the formation of the Scorpions they must now deal with civilians. In every era there would be some who could not be made to believe the evidence of their senses, some who could not be manipulated. The best men and women, the strongest, those were the ones that must be searched out, run to ground and eliminated. Quickly, he hoped, painlessly, but this was outside his control.

They had gone too far to turn back. Already Zebulon's son, an ordinary boy as he remembered with a simple American name, Jack was it? or Jim? had taken the name Zebulon as though it were an hereditary title that would pass from generation to generation, legitimizing their organization and its aims. His own son was looking at him strangely as though he were waiting for the day when he could call himself Boris, disturbed because the Americans already had exchanged their founder for a myth that would not interfere with the day-to-day decision making while the Russians were still burdened with a senile old man.

He had grown a pair of mustaches and wore puttees and a monocle, like the picture of his great grandfather or was it The Battleship Potemkin, he was remembering? The corrupt old officer who serves the men meat crawling with maggots and triggers a mutiny, the man whom the sailors murder and throw into the sea, did he look like him?

One of his grandchildren brought him a shell, Sergei, the one that he loved best, dressed in his sailor suit like a little Prince. "We did it for you, my little one, for you and all the rest that you might grow up healthy and strong in a world at peace." He held the child tight and covered him with kisses, his mustaches and wet old man's mouth rubbing the rosy cheeks until the boy squirmed loose and ran away.

Boris's eyes went back to the newspaper. The young Tsar and his pretty bride had given birth to another daughter, *little Anastasia. It would be three years before Alexei was born, poor little hemophiliac, how his mother fretted. She could have saved her tears. They would be gunned down, all of them in a heap in the cellar of the house in Ekaterinburg. The soldiers watching for the twitch of a limb ready to begin their manic firing again.*

There must be some way to prevent the bloodbath. The Tsar is a good man, but too easily influenced, not a bright man, it is true, but well meaning. If he can be steered away from war with the Japanese, if Rasputin never arrives in the capital, if we begin now to immerse him in the ways of socialism, if we whisper them in his ear, he and his family can be moved quietly into retirement. The little princesses—Olga, Tatiana, Marie, and Anastasia—if Boris closed his eyes he could see their sweet faces, could see them living on to maturity by the seaside.

"Look," one of the children pointed a chubby finger. "Grandpa is crying."

Boris opened his eyes. It was not the dead that he should dream of, but the living. Not the lives they had taken that mattered but the ones that he might still save.

Hieronymous Gartner put aside the papers. His own eyes were dry but his heart was hammering. How beautiful the woman had been and how well she understood him. But she played with ideas, shuffling and reshuffling, not recognizing her own death, not even when it was laid out before her.

He was an instrument of his times, an arrowhead whizzing through space ahead of the others. Not alone, merely at the forefront, blazing the path that others must follow. A tremor inside his breast pocket, the lightest vibration. His senses were so acute, that was enough. He reached inside for the wafer thin telephone. "Yes?" he was about to say but the voice at the other end anticipated him.

"I know you're there." It was the boy, his voice shrill with panic. "I know . . . who you are."

SIXTEEN

It was twentieth century week at the Codfish Club. There were ads in *The Reader*, posters all over the near north side. Anyone arriving in the costume of the featured decade was admitted free. Living in the basement of the church, just a few steps away from the donations room, Christian had no trouble recreating the 70's. Donny Osmond would have been proud of his pants and the psychedelic shirt with the long tabbed collar. Slater had been right. These clothes never die. Polyester is eternal.

He could do without the smell, though. These synthetic materials captured the aroma of the past and let it live on. If only Tess had known, polyester could have been the technology behind one of the Scorpion manipulations. Something as simple as burning old clothes could trigger a wave of noxious gas, which if administered in small enough quantities, could take us back in time. He sniffed inside his borrowed shirt. The full dose would probably kill you.

Tuesday, December 28, the Psychedelic Seventies. Two days since he climbed through the window of the church on Wood Street and fell into an exhausted sleep in the furnace room. Churches are quiet on Monday. He slept all day and woke when the women of the parish arrived to prepare the meal for the homeless, spaghetti with meatballs and plenty of bread. He couldn't believe his luck. He left with the others after the meal and prowled the streets looking for news.

He still had money. Money was not the problem, his pockets were full of it. But he had no clothes. He couldn't go back home and he had abandoned his car long ago or had it only been Saturday, Christmas, the day that he found Slater's body and stumbled off into a nightmare. Death was a plague that he carried. Everyone he talked to, everyone whose life he touched, they were all dying one by one. After he found Randall's body, he had spent the whole night walking north. He had cleaned up as best he could in the gas station rest room, waiting quietly until a customer emerged who was willing to hold the door open.

He stopped in Dunkin' Donuts and waited until it seemed late enough to call Helen Carver. Now he had just one call left. Monday night, his stomach full and the streets quiet, he reached his decision. There was only one man who could help him, one man whose reach was longer than the arm of the law, one man still left in this world who had a reason to help him.

Through all the terrors of the past few days he had

clung to the card that Hieronymous Gartner gave him, transferring it from pocket to pocket, touching it like a talisman to remind himself that he was not alone. On Monday night at 10:30 he found a bar without a television. It must be the only one left in the city and he was the only customer. The bartender nodded morosely as he entered. He was an old man with old ideas about how customers should be entertained and old prices still posted on the wall.

He shuffled over and asked Christian "What you want?" in an accent so thick, he could barely understand. "Beer," Christian told him, "Draft, one," and he raised his index finger in confirmation. The old man nodded and shuffled off, returning with a glass of flat lukewarm beer the color of pee. Christian took a drink and winced. The man watched him. "Good," he said, "Fine," reaching in his pocket and laying a dollar on the bar.

There was a sign in the center of the mirror advertising Miller's, the name Tony's written above it in neon script. "Tony?" he nodded to the bartender, raising his glass. The old man eyed him suspiciously. "Tony," he finally answered, then he shuffled off to get Christian's change.

This must be daycare, Christian thought, when Tony returned and laid a quarter and two dimes next to his glass. The family drops him off in the morning, maybe they stay long enough to help him open, then they pick him up at night. Somebody must stop by periodically to make sure he's still alive. But otherwise, what a setup. As soon as he dies, they'll sell it. "Nice location," he observed, raising his glass in Tony's direction.

Tony nodded. "No food. Pretzel, peanut, potato chip. No food."

Christian waited until the old man retreated to the far corner of the bar, before taking the card out of his pocket. He had waited a long time to ask for help. When he turned the card over, the final piece of the puzzle fell into place. 737-8260. The number that Gartner had written on the back of the card was the same as the number on his mother's calendar.

Christian could feel his eyes fill with tears. The man he was calling for help was not just his employer, with a vested interest in the virus and in everything that happened to his employees. He was his father.

Tony had an old fashioned booth in the back, with Telephone written in blue across the top. Christian ordered another beer and drank it quickly to still the trembling in his hands. He picked up the wet change from the bar, walked to the back of the room and shut himself into the booth.

"I know—I know who you are," he said before the man had a chance to answer.

"Good," the voice said. "I'm glad."

"I need your help."

"Tell me where you are."

Christian looked around the bar. Tony was staring out the window, so close to death it hardly mattered. On the other end of the line, Gartner was quiet, waiting. "The Codfish Club," Christian finally blurted.

"Give me the address."

Christian told him.

"We'll be there in 15 minutes, maybe less."

"Not today."

"What?"

"Tomorrow night at 10:30. Psychedelic night. It's crowded there. We'll be safe."

"All right."

"I tried to do it by myself," Christian took a deep breath, holding back the tears, "But I can't."

"It's all right, son." Gartner felt a single tear roll down his face. "You've been very brave."

Christian showered at the church, washing himself with liquid hand soap and drying off with brown paper towels. He wiped the water from the floor and tried to clean up after himself. This was the last night he would spend in the furnace room. He felt almost nostalgic as he dressed in his borrowed clothes.

He arrived early but there was already a line at the door. Two girlfriends in modern retro pants and platform sandals were arguing that they should get in free. The cashier told them to step aside and began talking to the next couple in line.

The line moved up. Christian wished he had time to grow sideburns. He was lucky he had been able to shave. Stubble had come in with Miami Vice in the late 80's. Very *un*-retro, dude. Totally. Good thing he had found a plastic throw-away razor in the church bathroom. It was dull but it got the job done.

The line moved up. It was the bouncer's job to scrutinize each of the patrons, to make sure that no one slipped in under age. Christian knew the drill. He had to show his driver's license and hope that the man wasn't interested enough to look closely, that he had been working so hard the past few days, he hadn't had time to glance at the television or read the paper. Christian had seen his face smiling back at him from the front page of the Sunday Tribune. "Police Seek Victim's Associate," the headline read. They had spelled his name wrong.

The line moved up. One more couple and it would be his turn. He rehearsed his moves, hold out the license, then make eye contact, nod nonchalantly, and move on.

The line moved up. He was on.

"Christian—what is that?"

"Wahrmutter," he whispered hoarsely.

"Is that German or something?"

Christian nodded.

"My grandfather came from Germany. Guggenhopf, that's my name. Doesn't mean anything. Just sounds goofy. What about yours?"

"What?"

"What does that mean—Wahrmutter?"

"True—" Christian cleared his throat. "True mother."

"Oh yeah? I wonder how they thought of a name like that?"

"Hey," somebody yelled from farther down, "Keep it moving."

The bouncer rolled his eyes. "Go on in, Christian," he waved away the ten dollar bill. "You're free. Cool threads."

Christian stopped in the bathroom first, to throw cold water on his face and wait for his heart to stop hammering. Someone else came in and he realized that he'd have to leave or risk becoming even more conspicuous. He longed for the comradery of the girl's john. You could hang out there all night, if you wanted. Sometimes they even had couches. Girls sat around putting on makeup, criticizing their dates, even sleeping it off. If you hung out too long in the men's room, somebody would either hit on you or beat you up. The guy at the urinal was sneaking looks at him, wondering why he was still here. He nodded briskly, a manly nod, and left.

The crowd at the bar was three deep. He edged in and ordered a Coors, because that was what the guy ahead of him ordered. Then he stepped back against the wall and looked around.

They had set up a special dance floor, just for the night, with squares of light flashing on and off under the dancers' feet. A big silver ball turned overhead, probably left over from "The Roaring Twenties." That would have been last Wednesday. He did the math quickly in his head. Tomorrow was the 80s, then the 90s. On New Year's Eve, they reprised all the decades at once.

The seventies were easy to recreate. The clothes still looked like new, even though they smelled bad. He saw five guys in John Travolta's white suit but none of them had the hair for it. Lots of girls in ruffled dresses, even more in clingy rayon with chokers, long hair parted down the middle. Actually, you could probably get away with your sixties outfit from the night before. He doubted that Guggenhopf was a stickler for details.

The clothes in the seventies had been darker, slinkier. The lines were pretty much the same, but the sixties were more innocent and colorful. People had fun in the sixties as they stumbled from one drugged out sexual experience to another. In the seventies, they settled in. The thrill was gone. Sex had moved from the campus to the suburbs. Become ordinary, sleazy. The children suffered.

He took a long pull on his bottle, hoping to shake the mood he had fallen into, as though the twentieth century were spread out before him and he was the judge. The emcee called for quiet and introduced the Codfish dancers. They were about to demonstrate "The Hustle." Three boys in tight pants and psychedelic shirts, wearing wigs, he was almost certain and false sidburns. took the center of the floor. Their partners had short skirts and platform heels and tight little tops with zippers. One girl had a lowcut, long sleeved jersey with fringe all over it, like Dolly Parton.

The crowd moved back to give them room. That was when he saw her. In a long scarlet sheath that clung to her slender frame, set off her white hair, made her eyes look enormous. She was leaning back quietly against her partner. Her hands holding his against her waist. The man leaned down to whisper something in her ear and she smiled. For a moment their two bright silvery heads caught the light. Julie leaning so seductively yet comfortably against Hieronymous Gartner.

"Hey, Christian!" Guggenhopf called after him. "Hey, where you going?"

The man's genial stupidity distracted him momentarily. He turned, just for a second, then ran across the street, directly into the path of a car. The driver slammed on his brakes and leaned on the horn. Christian kept running. There was nowhere left to go, all the more reason to run, from the police, from the encounter that he knew was coming, but mostly from himself.

"Tell me about your mother," she had said. He could see her saying it as she climbed on top of him, over and over, no matter how fast he ran. This was the reason for his blindness, the truth he had not wanted to see. The first death belonged not to Slater but to Tess and he had brought it.

"Tell me," she had moaned, working her hips, making him dance inside her.

The story had burst from him, gushed like pent up waters running from their source, running, running.

"It's about the Millennium," he could hear his own voice echoing inside his head. "And how it doesn't happen. We go back in time instead. Because of a virus or something that undoes all the Y2K programming."

She had laughed her silvery, little girl's laugh, like bells. He could still hear it. The memory made him dizzy while he leaned against the side of the building struggling to catch his breath.

People were walking around him, turning back to look curiously or with disapproval, wondering if they should stop. He could see a woman conversing animatedly with her husband, gesturing in his direction, telling him to do something.

"That's what we pay the police for," he heard the man say, taking the woman's hand firmly and pulling her away.

"Are you all right?" she called after Christian. "Should we call the police?"

"Fine, fine," Christian gasped, waving her away and attempting to stand and breathe normally. He was still leaning against the wall, hoping his breathing would return to normal when he saw the policeman step out of a doorway just ahead.

At first he panicked. His eyes scanned the street, frantically looking for somewhere to hide. Then he realized that Officer McAuliffe hadn't seen him, hadn't even looked in his direction. He had emerged from the doorway—it must have been a restaurant—there was a toothpick in his mouth—yawned, stretched, turned his back on Christian and continued down the street.

People were still walking around him. Maybe he had become invisible. Christian started to laugh, so hard that he soon found himself leaning against the wall again. It was the clothes that did it. Of course, McAuliffe hadn't recognized him. He looked like an extra from *Saturday Night Fever*. The officer's broad back was disappearing slowly up the street, swallowed by the crowds. Christian began to follow him, slowly turning a new idea over in his mind

Maybe he should talk to Officer McAuliffe. Where else could he go? Who else could he trust? He hadn't done anything wrong after all. What little evidence they had was circumstantial, left behind by the real killer. Surely the police would recognize that. They were experts in those things.

The man wasn't even in uniform. They could go somewhere and talk it over. McAuliffe would advise him.

The policeman knew that he wasn't a killer. He liked him. He had come to his mother's funeral. Christian walked faster, keeping the policeman in sight. He was afraid of startling him, afraid of triggering some good guy/bad guy reflex out here in the street, without a chance to explain. He wanted the policeman to see him before he spoke, to see that he was turning himself in, that he had no tricks up his sleeve. So he followed at a safe distance and waited for his chance.

McAuliffe was moving at a leisurely pace, stopping to peer in windows. He went inside a drugstore and Christian panicked, wondering if he should go in after him, afraid of being spotted before he was ready to make his move. But he came out almost immediately, carrying a small bag that he dropped into the pocket of his coat. Now he walked faster whistling.

He turned into a bar with a racing neon light. "Ands . . . Ifs . . . Buts" the sign said. Christian didn't have time to figure out what it meant. It was dark inside. The jukebox was blaring an obscure Barbra Streisand song from the 60s. Christian only knew it because it had been one of Tess's favorites. "I don't care much," young Barbra sang, "go or stay. I don't care very much either way." It took a minute or two for his eyes to adjust to the darkness. Then he spotted him, already at the far end of the bar, deep in earnest conversation.

"Officer," he called out as soon as he was within range, not wanting to startle him. "Officer McAuliffe!" All the conversation stopped. No one was making a sound except Barbra. "So if you kiss me, if we touch," she belted her words into the silence, then dropped her voice so that she seemed to be talking rather than singing. "Fair is fair, I don't care . . . very much!"

Everyone was looking at Officer Bernard McAuliffe. The man he was talking to had slid off the bar stool and was backing slowly toward the restroom. "Officer McAuliffe," Christian hurried up now that he had his attention. "I need to talk to you." Slowly, out of the corner of his eye, Christian realized that there was something unusual about this bar, but he couldn't quite put his finger on it.

"Fancy meeting you here, Christian." McAuliffe draped an arm around his shoulder and steered him toward a back table. "My friend and I will have two drafts," he called out to the bartender.

"There aren't any women in here," Christian said suddenly.

Detective McAuliffe nodded confidentially. "I know."

"Oh my god," Christian blushed. "You must be— Jesus, I was so worried about startling you that I never thought . . . Did I blow your cover?"

"Christian," he leaned across the table and spoke patiently, "the chances of anything of mine getting blown tonight are pretty slim, wouldn't you say?"

SEVENTEEN

"Well, that's my little secret," Officer McAuliffe waited for the bartender to set the beers down on the table and withdraw. "What's yours?"

The glass was frosty and the beer had a good thick head. Christian studied it for a moment. "I didn't do it."

McAuliffe nodded and sat forward, resting his chin on his hands. Christian realized he had never seen a man make that gesture, but that it was all right. He could feel himself relaxing as he talked. "I found Slater's body and I panicked. I can't tell you how awful that was."

"You don't have to."

"Were you on the scene?"

McAuliffe nodded. "Pretty grisly, even for a cop, I can tell you. There were several of us needed to be excused from that one."

"How could they do that to a man as big as Slater, without any sign of a struggle, without any . . . and just leave him to bleed like that. Would he . . . would he be conscious, do you think?"

"Not the way we are now, but, well, yes, probably. There wouldn't be much pain involved, once you get past the terror of it. Kind of a slow fade, like drowning. You just get weaker and weaker as the blood drains away . . . I'm sorry. You asked me."

"The body panicked me. At first I couldn't accept it. I could see it but I couldn't really take it in. And all that blood. On my hands and my clothes, all over the desk and the printouts. I tried to clean him up."

"We saw that. It's how we got your fingerprints."

"Then when I realized what I was actually doing, what was all over me, I got sick."

"We saw that, too. Not unusual, believe me."

"To tell you the truth I kind of blacked out. I wasn't asleep but I have absolutely no memory of how I got out of that building. When I came to, I was wandering around outside. Good thing it was dark because there was blood all over my clothes. I found a gas station with a bathroom and cleaned myself up."

"What time was that?"

"I don't know—a little after 6:00, I guess. There was a diner a couple blocks away. When I went in, the news was on."

"I take it you didn't call the police?"

Christian shook his head. "No, but somebody else did. The television showed Slater's body being removed and then my picture came on the screen."

"So you panicked again?"

"I decided there was only one man who could help me."

"Not good old Bernie McAuliffe, obviously."

"Hieronymous Gartner."

"The head of the Doomsday Group?"

"That's right." Christian took a long gulp of beer to give him courage. "And I think he might also be my father." It was the first time he had said it aloud and he felt a little thrill of pride, despite the circumstances.

"Your father? What makes you think that?" McAuliffe drained his beer and signalled the bartender. "Apart from some obvious thing like your mother told you."

"She didn't tell me. She never told me anything. I figured it out." He shook his head at the offer of another beer. "It's a pretty long story. Maybe I'd better just tell you what I did next."

"Fair enough."

"I called Thatcher Randall."

"The guy who buried your mother?"

"Yeah. I wanted to know who paid for the funeral"

McAuliffe cocked an eyebrow. "Not you?"

"Slater called the funeral home and told them that the Doomsday Group was taking care of everything. He even came to the wake and hung around, signed the guest book and everything, told me it was company policy."

"You didn't believe him?"

"Did you ever hear of a company that pays for the funerals of their employees' mothers?"

"Not as a matter of policy, but they might do it for

someone special, particularly someone involved in an important project."

"That's me, all right."

"You don't think you're special?" McAuliffe eyed him over the top of his glass.

"It's not that. It's just that . . . I wanted to know exactly how special. Who signed the check and whether it was a company or a personal account."

"And?"

"Well, I called Randall and he agreed to see me that night, right away. He said he'd check the files, that they sometimes made a copy of the check. But by the time I got there he was dead." McAuliffe seemed surprised. "You didn't know?"

"Sure, I heard, but I didn't know there was a connection to this case."

"I suppose it could be a coincidence, but that's not how it feels."

"So, you think you're Typhoid Mary?" McAuliffe swirled the remaining beer in the bottom of his glass. "Everyone you come in contact with, dies?"

"It's not funny."

"I don't imagine it is."

"My mother's agent, too. I called her in New York when my mother's system crashed to see if she had a copy of the story."

"She's dead, too?" McAuliffe was beginning to look interested.

"An accident on the turnpike."

"Oh well," McAuliffe set down his glass. "An accident."

"Something with the brakes. Don't you ever go to the movies?"

McAuliffe laughed. "Are you asking?"

Christian blushed. "I just meant that if this were a movie, the killer would have tampered with the brakes."

"Yeah, well, if this were a movie, I'd have better lines. Come on, drink up. We'll go for a walk."

"Are you taking me in?"

"Only if you're easy. I meant easily taken in, you know, a joke."

"What about this strikes you as funny, exactly? My mother's death? The death of my associates and friends? The days I've spent on the street running from the police?"

"Christian, look, I'm sorry. You've come to me for help, I know. Maybe I'm just glad to see you and I'm making jokes to cover how relieved I am, that you're safe."

"Aren't I a suspect?"

"No, you're not a suspect!" McAuliffe sputtered with indignation. "What do you take us for, a bunch of amateurs? Murderers don't try to clean up the victim and leave their prints all over the scene. Murderers, especially amateurs, you'll excuse the expression, don't slit people's throats. This is the work of a professional, someone with a lot of practice."

"And you don't think I killed Thatcher Randall?"

"Not unless you shot him with your finger."

"I could have a gun!"

"That's right," McAuliffe agreed, "you could. Do you?"

"No." Christian sounded childish, even to himself.

"I didn't think so. Now come on, let's go." McAuliffe stood and pushed his chair back.

"Where are we going?"

"Come on, Christian, don't sulk. You'll be suspected of something soon, I promise."

They walked to Starbucks and settled in a quiet corner, on one of the funny shaped couches. People were coming and going and no one seemed to pay them any mind. "Let me get this straight," McAuliffe sat back and stretched his legs. "Your mother was writing a story about 16 different ways to stop the Millennium. You think that she was killed because of that?"

"I think she must have stumbled on to some part of the story that was true. Something that had to do with the virus we found in the files."

"And you know that your mother was in touch with Gartner?"

"I found his number on her calendar."

"But you called him for protection?"

"I didn't think it had to do with the virus. I thought it was about being my father."

"And you thought he killed her—why? So he wouldn't have to admit that you were his son?"

"I thought—maybe you were right and she had died of natural causes. I thought—well, obviously I didn't think at all. I had finally stumbled on the one man who was supposed to protect me all my life. So I went to him for protection."

"It has a kind of psychological resonance,"

McAuliffe nodded sympathetically, "but I doubt the police would be interested, apart from myself, of course."

Christian shifted uncomfortably. "This is all speculation until we come to Slater's body."

"So why do you think Slater was killed?"

"At first I thought he was stealing gold and ran into the person responsible for the virus. Or maybe he was in on it from the beginning and this was some kind of double cross. But now I think it was because he read my mother's story."

"And Thatcher Randall?"

"Because he knew about the connection between Gartner and my mother."

"And you're still alive because Gartner is your father?"

Christian nodded glumly. When he put it like that, it sounded silly.

"Well," McAuliffe steepled his hands in front of his face.

"You don't believe me."

"I believe you. It's just that I don't know what to do with you. The easiest thing would be to lock you up. But I'm not sure I can convince anyone to hold you and I can't do it on my own authority. That means I've got to find some place to stash you, until we figure out what to do next."

"Do you live around here?"

McAuliffe grinned wickedly. "I thought you'd never ask."

Bernie McAuliffe lived on the fourth floor of an old red brick apartment building in the shadow of Wrigley Field. It was sparsely furnished, clean but not particularly homey. Christian guessed that it was not a place where McAuliffe spent much time. He sat on the couch and tried to make himself at home while the policeman foraged in the kitchen for food.

"Anything I can do?" he called out just as McAuliffe emerged carrying a tray with two white china cups, a jar of Nescafe and a Sara Lee coffeecake. "I put it in the oven to warm it up," he said as he inserted the knife and began to saw off two pieces. Either the inside was still frozen or he had microwaved it to death. Christian reached for the little white plate that held his piece.

"You know you were set up . . ." McAuliffe began after they had chewed for a while in silence. "But you don't know why . . ."

"It has something to do with the virus," Christian sucked daintily on a water-logged pecan, wondering how much he had to eat before he could politely put the plate down.

"And with your mother's story, or so you surmise, but it could also have something to do with the connection between you and Gartner . . . and your mother." McAuliffe sighed just as the kettle began whistling in the kitchen. "Excuse me."

"I know it sounds ridiculous." Christian called out. There was a picture of a fishing boat on the far wall. He got up to study it. Maybe McAuliffe had rented the furniture. He had never seen a place with so little personality.

"That picture came from my mother's house,"

McAuliffe said shyly as he entered with the kettle. Christian hurried over to the tray and began spooning coffee into the cups. "It hung over the couch in the living room for as long as I could remember. But I decided to put it over there where I could see it."

"It's lovely," Christian mumbled as he grayed his coffee with 2% milk. "Is your mother . . . ?"

"Gone," McAuliffe nodded, "when I was still in high school. She was an old woman by then. I'm the youngest of seven boys," he explained, "the baby."

"Are they all policemen?"

"No, most of them are in insurance like my father. I'm the only one on the force. I suppose I felt obliged to do something physically tough, because of, well . . ."

It was strange how quickly McAuliffe had become shy in his own house. "Your place is very masculine looking," Christian added as though McAuliffe were suppressing an instinct for decoration out of deference to his family.

McAuliffe thanked him, then lapsed into silence.

"I know that everything I've told you sounds like a kind of paranoid fantasy," Christian broke the silence.

"It's not that—"

"I wouldn't believe it myself if it weren't for the bodies."

"I believe you. I'm just wondering how much of it I could make a judge believe. Whether we should try to swear out a warrant or just keep poking around on our own."

"It would help if we could find Julie." Christian ignored the sympathy in McAuliffe's eyes. "She might be able to tell us . . . something . . . about Gartner's activities."

"You must be tired," McAuliffe put his cup down and picked up the tray. "There's a towel and a toothbrush for you in the bathroom."

He awoke to the sound of McAuliffe's alarm. He kept his eyes closed while the shower was running and while McAuliffe padded around the kitchen. He smelled coffee and heard the policeman pour cereal into a bowl. He still had his eyes closed when he heard him undoing the locks on the front door.

When he woke up, the telephone was ringing. "Christian," he could hear McAuliffe's voice on the answering machine, "it's me. Pick up the phone." Christian stumbled off the couch and found the receiver.

"Good morning, sleepy head."

"What time is it?"

"Eleven thirty," the policeman chuckled.

"I meant to get up as soon as you left."

"I know. I could hear those little wheels turning. But I figured you'd fall back asleep as soon as I was gone."

"Are there any new developments?"

"No. I just called to tell you that there's coffee in the kitchen in the cabinet over the sink and bacon and eggs in the refrigerator. I keep the bread in the freezer."

"Thanks."

"Fix yourself some breakfast. Watch a little television. The paper is right inside the door. I should be back around 4:30."

"Sure, but I thought I'd—"

"Whatever you do, don't go out."

"Yeah, but—"

"No but's. Sit tight until I get there."

It was surprisingly easy to get into the building. A middle-aged man held the door for him while he pretended to fumble for his keys. "Thank you," he said trying not to make eye contact as he rushed past him to the third floor. They could be one of those two income households with the child in daycare and the mother and father at work. If they were, the apartment would be empty. Perhaps there was something to be gained by picking the lock and exploring for himself.

If he knew how to pick a lock, that is. He tapped softly on the door. His best bet was to find the father gone to work and the mother home alone with the child. He was good with children, after all, and charming—or at least not intimidating—to women.

The door opened before he was ready, before he had settled on a plan. "Madame Lemereaux . . . ?" he began. The woman's eyes were wary. "Who are you?" she asked. There was a sudden commotion behind her. "Maman—"

"Not now, Juliette—" she turned to address the child.

Christian could see a small pair of chubby legs behind Madame Lemereaux. A blond curly head poked its way around her mother's legs. "Papa!" the voice crowed.

"No, Juliette!"

The little girl raced into the hall and clutched Christian's legs, laughing with delight. "Papa!" she said, laughing and dodging her mother's arms. "Papa!"

"Madame Lemereaux, please," Christian begged,

while he struggled to entangle the child's hands from the legs of his pants. "Just a minute of your time, a very few questions. Out here in the hall, if you wish."

The little girl was sitting between his legs, holding on to his pants and laughing. He reached down gently and entangled her chubby little fingers, scooped her up and passed her without hesitation to her mother. "Please, Madame Lemereaux, just for a few minutes."

The woman looked him up and down. Her face was impassive but relaxed, now that she held the child. "Very well," she said, stepping aside to let him enter.

The first thing that he saw was a photograph sitting on a small table beneath a lamp. It showed Julie, *his Julie*, holding the child and smiling at the camera.

They sat in the kitchen. Madame Lemereaux had made a pot of chocolate for herself and the child. He sat down and she passed him a cup.

"Her name is Abigail," she said, "Abigail Dussant."

The picture stood between them on the table. Julie's hair was longer, less fashionable, but otherwise, she was the same.

The little girl sat in the middle of the floor, feeding her teddy bear with a small plastic spoon. Once she came over and offered it to him. He smacked his lips. "Oh yes," he said, "very good."

Madame Lemereaux smiled. "You miss Abby, don't you, darling? She was very good with my daughter. Julie loved her."

"How long did she live with you?

"Nine months. She gave no trouble, was always

good with the child. Then one day she came to me, said she was going back to Montreal, that her father was ill and she must leave immediately. Just like that and she was gone."

"Did she leave an address, a telephone number?"

"Yes, but they're no good. The telephone has been disconnected. We sent a letter to the address and it came back marked 'Unknown.' We did not know what to think, my husband and I. But we decided that we would not take another *au pair* into our home, no matter how well recommended. Instead I stay at home with the child while my husband goes to the university. It is hard because I make no friends, but soon Juliette will be old enough for school, then perhaps . . ." She brushed the little girl's curls with her hand.

"And you know nothing else about her, Madame? Jobs she may have held? The names of her friends?"

The woman shook her head. "I'm sorry, M'sieur. I know so very little. My husband and I have been very foolish. Because she spoke good French, we imagined that we could trust her. But wait, there is one thing." She stood up excitedly and left he room. When she came back she was carrying a little card. "We found this in her room."

"History Repeats Itself?" he read the name on the card.

"It is a vintage clothing boutique. Perhaps they know her there."

He pocketed the card. "Perhaps." The address was on Damen Avenue, near the Codfish Club.

EIGHTEEN

A life-size photo of Ida McKinley entering a ball-room hung suspended in the window. A mannequin stood beside the picture wearing a copy of the McKinley ball gown. In the second window, another mannequin was dressed to look like Marilyn Monroe. A system of thin wires held her dress suspended in the air as she stepped over the manhole. Christian shaded his eyes and peered inside. The shop looked empty. History Repeats Itself: Authentic Vintage Clothes and Period Pieces Made to Order. Christian pressed the handle and went in.

The bell on the door played *Auld Lang Syne* but no one stepped out from behind the curtain to serve him. In the front of the store were racks of authentic vintage clothes, shoes and accessories. In the back near the changing rooms was a rack of sample made-to-order pieces flanked by bolts of material. The floors were hardwood, the walls white and Spartan. Here and there a sepia photo tinted in bright unnatural color. A modern chair with Mission lines. A hexagonal table stripped down to natural oak then bleached to rob it of all color. This is background, the decor seemed to say. You make the statement.

Christian was admiring an Edwardian tea gown when he heard rustling behind him. "May I help you?" the voice said. He turned quickly.

She was wearing a silver lamé flapper dress. Her hair had been dyed a shiny patent leather black and her mouth carefully painted a bright candy apple red. Christian would have known her anywhere. "Hello, Julie," he said, "Or would you prefer Abigail?"

The color faded from her face and the perfect made-to-order smile disappeared. She thought about running. He saw her gasp and take a step back, her eyes scanning the room wildly, hoping for a hiding place. Then she saw it was no good. She turned her head and put her hands out in front of her, as though begging him to stop for a minute, reconsider. He thought he heard her say please.

He slapped her as hard as he could, his hand moving through the air with all the force of his will behind it. Her head seemed to snap at the moment of impact and her knees gave way beneath her. He thought about the windows behind him, exposing him to the street. He seized her wrist, just as she crumpled and dragged her back behind the curtain. She made no resistance, only crouched with her hands over her head to protect herself.

He reared back ready to kick her, when he saw his reflection on the far wall. The man in the mirror was a madman, face contorted with rage. Christian gasped and turned to see if someone had come in behind him. Then he dropped to his knees and began to sob. She crawled away and sat at a safe distance watching him. "Are you going to kill me?" she said finally.

"Why?" he said when he was finally able to speak. "Why did you do it?"

"For the money." Her voice was perfectly flat and devoid of any emotion.

"And your son? What about him?"

"I have no son. Everything I have in the world is here in this shop. He gave it to me. He took out his checkbook and signed a blank check and gave it to me. He told me I could have whatever I wanted. I said there was only one thing: this shop. He laughed and said I'd have a hundred shops like this. I'd invent *haute couture*. Coco Chanel would be nothing, a little shop girl. It would be me they sang about."

Christian stopped crying and turned to stare.

"I didn't know what he meant, not for a long time. And then it was too late." Her voice fell.

"What are you talking about?"

She cringed, afraid of his interest, his sudden attention.

"Julie, Abby, it's all right." He was kneeling beside her. "I won't hurt you, I promise. Just tell me."

"I didn't know about your mother until after. I swear it. I didn't know. If it hadn't been me, it would have been someone else, some other hungry girl."

"What, Julie? What are you talking about?" He had

an urge to grab her shoulders and shake the truth out of her.

"You don't know?" He shook his head and her eyes grew big. She beckoned him closer. "He's taking us back in time, all of us." Her voice dropped. "Just like in your mother's story."

McAuliffe began yelling as soon as he opened the door. "Are you crazy?" he said. "Are you trying to get yourself killed and me thrown off the force?"

Christian put a finger against his lips. "Not now," he said. "I brought someone with me." He pushed Julie into the room and closed the door carefully behind them. "This is the girl I told you about. She has something to tell you."

Julie huddled in the center of the room shivering in spite of her white rabbit fur coat.

"Why is she shaking like that?" McAuliffe studied her.

"It's cold out. And she's nervous. Stop staring at her."

"Looks like someone roughed her up a little." McAuliffe tilted her chin. "What is it, baby? You need something?"

Her eyes widened. She looked as though she were about to speak.

"Just get her a cup of tea," Christian said. "She'll be fine."

"All right." McAuliffe disappeared into the kitchen.

Christian settled Julie in the center of the couch and

unbuttoned her coat. "You want to take it off?" She shook her head and folded her arms in front of her chest. "Come on, just like this," Christian pried her fingers from the edges of the fur coat. "See, we'll drape it like this, around your shoulders." He could hear McAuliffe putting a tray together in the kitchen.

"It's all right," he said, stroking her cheek. He could feel her beginning to relax under his fingers. "Everything will be all right."

The kettle whistled shrilly in the kitchen and just as abruptly stopped. By the time McAuliffe reentered with the tray, Julie was leaning back against the couch.

"Here we are," the policeman set the tray down gently in front of her on the coffee table. Milk, sugar, three cups and a little saucer of lemon slices. "I didn't know how you take it so I brought in everything." He returned to the kitchen and came back with a plate of Girl Scout cookies.

Christian poured while Julie nibbled daintily on a vanilla sandwich cookie. She added milk and sugar to her tea, stirring carefully as though she were following a precise recipe. Then she took a long drink, set the cup down and began to speak.

"I met Hieronymous Gartner three years ago at the Codfish Club. I was working there as a—a dancer." She dropped her eyes and began to twist her hands nervously in her lap. Christian sat forward but McAuliffe waved him back. "Go ahead," he said sitting forward attentively, "we understand."

"Sometimes the club would be rented out for private parties. We'd do our show and afterwards some of the girls would be asked to stay. The boys sometimes, too, depending on the guests' preference." She shivered and pulled the coat around her.

"One night the club was rented out for a Prohibition Party. The guests were all older men, wealthy they told us. Most of them were dressed like gangsters. Nothing happened," she added hastily. "We sat around on their laps while they got drunker and drunker. All except one. He sat in the corner all night, just watching. When everybody fell asleep, he paid us off and sent us home in cabs."

"That was Gartner?"

Julie nodded. "Just as we were leaving he spoke to me. His voice was different, soothing somehow, almost hypnotic. He told me that he noticed me. I stood out from the others, he said. I had a special 'quality' he called it. I never quite knew what he meant. He asked me if I wanted to . . . stay with him. I said no. I was a dancer, not a—" She blushed and McAuliffe nodded, sitting forward more intently, as though he understood.

Christian had gotten up and was standing in front of the window, staring down at the street, pretending not to listen.

"He said it was all right. He didn't mind. That just proved how special I was. Then he touched me, ever so lightly, on the arm and I felt . . . I can't describe it . . . it was like electricity. He said that he often had little parties like this. He and his friends liked to dress up in costumes and sometimes they took pictures. He asked me if I'd like to join them sometimes. He'd send a car for me.

"I said yes. He had moved his hand so that it was resting on the base of my spine. I would have said yes to anything. That's how it started. I saw him twice that week. And the next time he asked me to stay, I did. I never went back.

"He liked that I knew all about fashion, how people dressed at the turn of the century and what their houses looked like. He said that someday we'd all live like that again. There was no progress, he said. The world just moved in cycles. It looked as though things changed, but they really didn't. If you waited they would come full circle. The trick was to stay on top, no matter what. I didn't really know what he meant. But it sounded right somehow, like something your mother would say to you or your father. Some old truth that you'd never forget.

"About a year ago he came to me with a proposition. He had talked about setting me up in business. Giving me my own shop. He said he had found just the right place for me. He took me to a little vintage clothing shop on Damen. He said he was buying the owner out. There was a little deli next door and he bought that, too, and knocked the wall out. He told me to fix the place, gave me carte blanche. He offered to bring in a decorator from New York, but I said no. I knew what I wanted. I knew where to get it all, too, and cheap. He smiled when I said that. He said that nothing good ever came cheap and someday I'd realize that. But he let me do whatever I wanted. He didn't try to interfere.

"By the time I was finished I had a place that was special. Three girls worked for me and we couldn't keep up with the orders. I had to farm them out, to foreign women because they could sew anything and they worked so cheap. I fixed up a room for them in the basement. He laughed and said I was reinventing the sweat shop. But I didn't care what he said. I had the best place in the city. There were a lot of boutiques that sold antique clothes, but I made my own patterns and helped women put together a vintage look of their own. Men, too. He ordered things from me himself.

"Then slowly my clientele began to change. He began bringing people to my shop, the wives and girl friends of the men he had with him that first night at the Codfish Club. The clothes that they ordered all came from the same period: the turn of the century. He showed me photographs and gave me a list of acceptable materials. I didn't think anything of it at first. He was my benefactor and these were his friends. Then one day he showed up with a tall thin-lipped woman in an Edwardian suit. My new manager, he said, someone to run the business for me while I was away 'on assignment.'

"He told me I had to leave the shop temporarily and go to work for one of his companies. There was a young man there and I was instructed to make contact with him and find out all I could about the project he was working on. He coached me himself on what I should say and do." She sat with her head bowed, like a flower with a broken stem. Christian was looking down on the street, his back ramrod straight, the back of his neck flushed.

"That's when you met Christian?" McAuliffe prompted.

She nodded, her head drooping, her hair covering her face. "He never told me why he wanted the information and I didn't ask. When I heard that Christian's mother was dead, I—" she covered her face with her hands. When she looked up finally, she was white as a sheet. "May I—may I have a glass of water?"

It was Christian who brought her the water. "It's all right," he said, "you don't have to talk any more. We know the rest."

"I need to say it," she spoke in a quiet voice. "I need to make it real." She drained the glass he had placed beside her, took a deep breath and began again. "I tried to leave him then, but it was too late. I contacted an aunt in Montreal and told her I was coming. I made my plans in secret and the night before I was supposed to leave, I got a telegram. My aunt had been in a terrible accident. She was paralyzed. He was very kind, offered to fly me down or have her transferred to a nursing home here in Chicago. I never tried to leave again. It was easier to do what he wanted."

She slept like a child, her face flushed, her breath deep and even, a little bubble of saliva forming at the corner of her mouth. Christian hovered over her, pulling the afghan over her shoulders, patting her back. "She didn't know," he said, rejoining McAuliffe at the window. "How could she know?"

McAuliffe nodded, avoiding his eyes.

"Gartner will be waiting with his friends at Glessner House, tomorrow night. This gives you the information you need to swear out a warrant."

McAuliffe poured a snifter of brandy. "Drink this, Christian."

Christian waved the glass away. "I know it's hard to believe—"

"What possible reason would he have for wanting us to go back in time?"

He wants to be an honest-to-god tycoon, like J.P. Morgan and Andrew Carnegie."

"But how?"

"Why is that so important? The man is a murderer. He's trying to suppress my mother's novel. He doesn't care so much that Slater and I found the virus. He's betting that we don't have enough time or enough brain power to figure out what it's really there for. He wants to make sure that no one even thinks about the possibility of time travel between now and New Year's Eve."

"The police are cordoning off Prairie Avenue for the Party of the Century."

Christian looked up hopefully.

"I already spoke to my chief. They're dressing in costume, acting as security. All the big wigs are scheduled to be there. With their wives and their jewelry. As well as anyone else with the money for a ticket."

"Slater got us passes," Christian broke in excitedly. "As employees of the Doomsday Group, we're entitled to spend the night at Glessner House. The other guests will be shuffled down the street to places like Clarke House. But we get to stay near Julie and Gartner. They're dressing as President and Mrs. McKinley."

"It will be a simple enough matter to put on some extra cops and to keep a close watch on Gartner for the evening. I've already talked to the chief. It's a pretty low risk since we'll already be there anyway. But you've got to understand how strange this whole story sounds and how embarrassing it would be for the department—"

"I do understand. I'll do anything you say, I promise. I'm just glad that you're taking this seriously. Glad that we have you on our side."

"There's something else you need to understand. About Julie. She's not as free as she sounds."

"Gartner is a genius. He hypnotizes people. You can't hold that against her."

"Didn't you see the marks on her arms?"

"When I first saw her, I went a little crazy, I—"

McAuliffe shook his head. His eyes were sad. "I'm talking about needle tracks, Christian. It must be hard to reform when you have such an expensive habit."

"How many Ida McKinley's can you have at one party?" McAuliffe was peering nervously through the curtain. They were standing in the back of History Repeats Itself, waiting for Julie to finish taking care of a customer. The shop was busy on New Year's Eve. People were coming and going. Many of them picking up the outfits they planned to wear this evening at Glessner House.

"Strictly speaking, they're not all Ida McKinley. Her dress was white. They're just using the pattern as a point of departure but they're making it in all different colors and adding features." Christian was pulling on a dark wig that gave him a wild-eyed look. "What do you think?" He turned to McAuliffe. "Do I look like an anarchist assassin?"

"Which one?"

"Doesn't matter which one. The one who shot McKinley was actually very wholesome looking and clean-shaven. The country was crawling with anarchists and secret societies, some of them dedicated to stomping out militarism. The police lumped them all together as anarchists but I bet we'd call some of them pacifists."

"My sideburns are too long," McAuliffe tried to pull one of them forward but the glue had already taken hold. He was going as a Pinkerton. "The only way I'll ever make detective," he had muttered. "After this little caper my career will definitely be over."

The curtain parted and Julie came back into the room. She was dressed in a peach-colored Edwardian tea gown that accented the delicacy of her complexion. Her hair was pulled back away from her face and a hairpiece anchored at the back of her head. Her eyes were enormous. Christian looked as though he were seeing her for the first time. "Traffic is getting heavier," she consulted the watch that hung from her waist. "They're sending the carriage for me at 5:30. I still have to get into my Ida McKinley dress."

"You're much more beautiful than Ida McKinley," Christian said, "She was a middle aged woman in 1900. President McKinley was dedicated to his wife. Did you know that?"

McAuliffe shook his head but Christian wasn't paying attention. He had his arms around Julie's waist. "He insisted that they be seated together, even at State Dinners, against all precedent."

"Mrs. McKinley was a very fragile woman," McAuliffe said.

"When McKinley was shot that was the first thing he worried about. Not his own health but Ida's. 'Be careful how you tell her,' he said as they carried him out. 'Be careful how you tell her.'"

McAuliffe looked away. When he turned back Julie was studying her face in the mirror. "I'll have to redo my hair," she said to herself as though she had forgotten they were still there. Then she gave her head a little shake. "It's time for you to go."

She opened the doors of a pine armoire that stood against the far wall. "I've got a pair of heavy wool great-coats for you." She took the darkest one off its wooden hanger and helped Christian into it. "This should keep you nice and warm." Then she handed the other coat to McAuliffe. "Be careful," she pressed her cheek against Christian's, then led them both to the door.

Christian wanted to linger but McAuliffe pulled him away. There was a hansom cab waiting for them at the corner. When they looked back she had already locked the door and posted the closed sign in the window. They climbed into the cab and set off for the Glessner House.

NINETEEN

The street lamps were just coming on as the cab pulled into Prairie Avenue. The policeman who stopped their carriage sported handlebar mustaches and a Keystone Cops helmet. McAuliffe flashed their invitation. The policeman gave a nod and a wink as he stuck his head inside the carriage. "Good Evening, sor," his brogue was thick enough to cut with a knife.

"Good evening, McNamara."

"Sure and it's a pleasure to be serving the quality instead of chasing the criminal element on a night like this."

"Go on with you, lad," McAuliffe bantered in return. "Keep your eyes open and your mouth shut."

"You can rest easy, sor. It's covering your back we'll be this long night . . . and waiting for your signal."

The officer gave a little salute as he closed the carriage door and thumped on the box for the driver to walk on.

McAuliffe fingered his lapel where the tiny microphone had been concealed. The grounds were swarming with police. Christian caught himself wondering how often the Scorpions had encountered armed resistance and whether all of the policemen he saw around him really were policemen.

"What are you thinking?" McAuliffe asked as their carriage passed through the arch and entered the brick courtyard.

"That my mother would have enjoyed all this," he said almost without thinking.

McAuliffe had time to pat his hand before they stepped out of the carriage.

Glessner House sat like a small fortress on the corner of 18th and Priairie. Built in 1887, the grim granite exterior, its face closed to the street, was a reminder of the uneasy truce between rich and poor following the Haymarket Riots. The wealthy Chicagoans who lived on Prairie Avenue during the Gilded Age were aware of the dangers but chose to tough it out for the convenience of being near the center of the city. Ironically, the Fort Dearborn Massacre had taken place nearby in 1812, just a scant 75 years before. Standing like an island in the middle of a risky-looking neighborhood in which light industry mixed with the homes of the very poor, the houses on Prairie Avenue were still a monument to the violence that lay just under the surface of city life.

The interior of Glessner House was a study in contrasts. Unlike other houses built to trumpet their owners' wealth, it had the cozy feel of a wood-paneled cottage, full of charming nooks that invited conversation or repose. Because of its intimate layout, other restored houses had been thrown open to accommodate the overflow. The result would be a giant turn-of-the-century block party. Coachmen were already warming themselves around little charcoal braziers and a bunch of raggedy boys costumed—Christian hoped—to look like urchins were building a bonfire at the other end of the street

Hieronymous Gartner would receive his guests here at Glessner House, then send them on to various locations, depending on the size of their donation. Christian had been expecting a receiving line inside the large wood-paneled entrance hall but he was told by a liveried butler, who bore a strong resemblance to the Director of Human Resources, that President and Mrs. McKinley had not yet arrived.

"Very authentic, sir," he murmured as he helped McAuliffe off with his greatcoat, "but if you don't mind, I'll have to collect your gun."

"I'm a Pinkerton detective. How can I function without my gun?"

"You'll just have to imagine that you have one, sir." The butler reached a practiced hand inside McAuliffe's jacket and removed a small pistol. "Security, sir. There's a lot of fine jewelry here this evening." The microphone wire came trailing out behind the pistol. "Sorry, sir," he smiled as he patted McAuliffe's lapel. "I seem to have dislodged your Walkman."

"No problem," McAuliffe ripped the rest of the

wire free and handed it to the butler. "Just waiting for the football scores."

The butler bowed slightly and ushered them into the study where some twenty people were already waiting. They were admiring each other's clothes in high-pitched excited voices. The party was just beginning. Little bursts of self-conscious laughter mingled with the sounds of the band tuning up on the landing in the hall.

"I thought you said it was wireless," Christian muttered as soon as the butler was out of earshot.

"Budgetary constraints," McAuliffe smiled and bowed to a woman in a headdress topped with ostrich feathers.

"Sir Lionel Wisdom," a British voice boomed behind them and a monocled man stuck out his hand.

"Bernard McAuliffe and Christian Wahrmutter, at your service, sir," McAuliffe made a little bow. "If I might add," he pressed the man's hand warmly, "we're all hoping for the relief of Mafeking."

"Damned topical, old boy," Sir Lionel winked and the monocle popped out of his eye.

"One of ours," McAuliffe smiled as Sir Lionel headed toward the punch bowl.

Christian nodded and tried to recover his composure.

"Relax," McAuliffe whispered, "that was only my toy gun." He bowed as a big-bosomed woman in full sail bore down upon them. "Margaret Dumont, I presume?"

Christian had no heart for mingling so he installed himself behind a potted palm. The band struck up a waltz and he amused himself by speculating how many of the dancers were members of a secret society dedicated to holding back the Millennium. He noticed other men standing like him at the edge of the dance floor. Were they part of the security force or some other more sinister brand of enforcer?

"Would you like to dance?" The voice in his ear made him jump. He turned to see a tall, woman in an Edwardian suit. "I'm a Suffragette," she said grimly and he realized that he had been staring.

"Yes, of course, I'm an anarchist." He planted a firm hand in her back and did his best to sweep her out on to the floor. They two-stepped for a while in silence. "I work for Mr. Gartner," Christian said uneasily. The woman barely nodded. Despite his best efforts to lead, Christian could feel himself being steered towards a curtained alcove.

The woman's grip on his shoulder was like iron. He realized too late that the grim set of her mouth came not from counting out the measures of the waltz but from determination to whisk him out of sight. They were engaged in a polite form of wrestling just outside the heavy velvet draperies when he felt a light tap on his shoulder.

"May I?" Before she could object, McAuliffe had cut in and was steering the iron maiden back toward the center of the room, where another burlier man cut in and waltzed her off the floor.

"That little woman was quite an armful," Christian said as McAuliffe made his way back through the crowd.

"That little woman was a man," he replied dryly, nodding to someone across the room. Christian looked across the dance floor in time to see Sir Lionel Wisdom disappear into the growing crowd.

At 9:00 a ripple of excitement passed over the dance floor. President and Mrs, McKinley were arriving. The sound of their carriage could be heard as it passed through the cobbled arch and into the courtyard. A group of men in period suits with stiff celluloid collars had appeared near the door. Secret service men to guard the president from anarchists perhaps or part of McAuliffe's force making sure that Gartner actually stepped into the trap. If need be, they could take him now as he entered to a burst of applause, Julie clinging to his arm, looking every bit as neurasthenic as Ida McKinley herself.

Gartner was in evening dress with a long dark cape flung around his shoulders. His hair shone silver in the light. He and McKinley were of an age but twentieth century nutrition and a regimen of fitness kept Gartner in his prime while the president had been a portly old man at the same age. Gartner flashed strong white teeth and leaned down smiling to whisper something in Julie's ear while he waved to the crowd. She smiled up at him shyly with a child's delight in her eyes.

"My friends," he raised his voice and the crowd fell silent. "We are gathered here this evening to celebrate a century of progress. With God's help we have learned the lessons of history. As the old century ends and a new one begins, we pledge to protect the resources of this great country while moving forward under the banner of technology into a bright future. On behalf of Mrs. McKinley and myself," there was a light ripple of laughter as he bowed solemnly in Julie's direction, "I welcome you to the Party of the Century!"

The band began to play and Gartner waltzed Julie into the center of the room. Christian turned away, unwilling to see the naked adoration in her eyes. Liveried servants circulated with drinks on silver trays. He grabbed one and downed it without thinking. "Compliments of Mr. McKinley," the white gloved servant bowed and backed away.

The music stopped and the dance floor emptied as the guests lined up to shake hands with the president. Gartner was flanked by a cadre of secret service. Julie stood by his side looking dazed and vacant. As the guests shook first Gartner's hand and then Julie's, they were skillfully maneuvered into the hall where servants waited to help them into their coats and usher them back outside into the frosty night air.

When the goats had been separated from the sheep and sent on their way to other houses where the beer came in glass bottles and the wine, although it continued to flow, was the type that could be purchased in any supermarket, servants closed and barred the massive front door. The band continued to play and Julie and Gartner moved among their guests, chatting animatedly, but the atmosphere had changed. The room was filled with bustle and anticipation. Christian was reminded of a city under siege.

The lights were dimmed. It would be more accurate to say that they were replaced. A discreet army of servants moved around the edges of the crowd, wheeling silver carts loaded with candelabra and kerosene lamps that they set out around the room.

As he looked around he could see that the composition of the crowd had also changed. The men looked older, sleek and self-satisfied. With their bushy whiskers and dark evening clothes, they resembled so many walruses. The women were of two types, long-limbed doe-eyed Gibson girls and stately matrons of the Margaret Dumont variety.

When the party began, he had noticed guests costumed in every era of the twentieth century. Elvis, Zorro and Andy Warhol rubbed elbows with both Roosevelts, Admiral Dewey and Carmen Miranda. As the evening wore on, the dress of the other decades had been gradually replaced with early nineteenth century. "Something is wrong," he turned to remark to McAuliffe but the words wouldn't come out.

The lights had become too bright and the music was giving him a headache. "You're sweating," McAuliffe frowned, his face distorted like a fun house mirror.

"Have to lie down," Christian stumbled toward a curtained alcove, hoping that McAuliffe would follow. "Excuse me," he muttered to the man already inside, perched at an odd angle on the settee with his head pitched forward.

As he reached out to touch the man's shoulder, he recognized the policeman with the thick brogue who had welcomed them at the gate. In the split second before the body lolled forward and on to the floor, he realized that the man's throat had been cut.

Where had it all gone wrong?
Zebulon stood with his hands behind his back staring

*down at the crowds milling outside his window. New Year's Eve
1999, 10:30 p.m. Most of the Scorpions were in bed at desig-
nated historical sites, tucked in by maids and menservants who
would shortly retire to administer their own sedatives.*

*In prior eras it had seemed necessary to see out the
Event, to watch from protected locations, strapped into viewing
chairs in front of large triple glazed windows, like travelers in a
primitive space craft. It had taken many eras to realize that the
Event itself was better unobserved. To drift off to sleep in one
century and awake in the next, to lift one's kerchiefed or night-
capped head off the pillow to the sound of sleigh bells in clear
frosty air and the servant rapping at the door. Happy New Year,
the maid would call as she carried in the tray, with the newspaper folded to show the date on the front page, January 1, 1900.*

*Only Zebulon himself must keep watch in the Hall of the
Ancestors, a skeleton security force discreetly patrolling outside
the door. The walls were hung with the portraits of his predecessors. Zebulon the Great, who lost his life in the first Manipulation and all those who came after and were given his name. They
spoke to him in many voices but their message was always the
same.*

"The future is in your hands, Zebulon."

*"No man approaches this moment without a certain re-
gret, a tinge of sadness."*

"For the sake of the others, you must bear it."

"You must watch through the night with us."

"No one on Earth knows your pain as we do."

"We alone can help you to bear it."

*He had been reading the memoirs of Zebulon the Wise,
trying not to think of the RTN Leaders strapped down in Belle-*

vue, injected with a serum that would carry them through the night so that they awakened to the nightmare world of an early twentieth century madhouse, without drugs, without understanding, without hope . . .

Zebulon shuddered. He was essentially a man of peace and it was this tolerance, this willingness to understand that had brought about the present crisis. The RTN uprising should have been nipped in the bud as the right wing advised. "There is always some opposition, my boy," his grandfather had told him. "You must crush it," the man had drawn his palsied hand into a fist, "before it crushes you."

They forgot that his beloved Mara had been one of the leaders. How could he silence the voice of his soul? Was he not obliged to listen and consider? Were not they all?

His eyes scanned the crowd, hoping against hope that she was still at large, that she had given up her goal of alerting the media. "Destroy your computers," he could still hear her shrill voice coming from the loud speakers, see her face on television, the fist upraised, the eyes flashing in triumph. "Destroy your computers before they destroy you," she had warned. "Destroy your computers while you can remember how to use them. Destroy—"

Then the screen had gone black and the guard had begun their house to house search for the members of the terrorist group who had taken over CNN headquarters. In the confusion of the media disruption and the simultaneous media coverage of the disruption, she had somehow slipped away. Sirens still whistled in the streets. He could hear them even behind the triple glazed windows.

The crowd should have dispersed by now, gone to join one of the free New Year's Eve parties sponsored around the city by the Scorpions. Experience had taught them that it was better to keep the crowds contained, drinking and celebrating, largely unaware of what was going on around them. Toward the end of the Old Time, the custom of holding non-alcoholic First Night parties had become popular. This was a trend that was easily suppressed by making unlimited quantities of alchohol available in each major city. The cost was nothing compared to the ease with which people could be rounded up afterwards and any disorientation experienced the next morning ascribed to hangover.

Zebulon smiled grimly. From his perch on the top floor of Scorpion headquarters in Times Square, the crowd looked very foolish. Sometimes it seemed that mankind did not deserve to live. The idea had certainly been whispered in his ear by several of the extreme right brethren. But they were known universally despite their large personal fortunes as fanatics and ultimately fools. Wiping out anyone not intelligent enough to make cause with the Scorpions would eliminate the population problem, it's true. Unfortunately it would also eliminate the work force.

The Leader of the Scorpions, the annointed Zebulon had to be wise enough to understand that. Their recipe for preserving mankind must include equal parts of independent free-thinking, which by rights belonged to the educated upper classes, the Scorpions, as well as a kind of insect intelligence, the kind that made bee hives and ant colonies such interesting manifestations of socialization. Cooperation and division of labor flourished in these lower societies despite the limited intelligence of the inhabitants or as some said, because of it.

His eye was drawn to some commotion down in the square. The people seemed to have flocked around the old Times building. There must be some special Millennium message being displayed. Zebulon peered through the telescope. It did not reflect the latest technology but it had been installed by one of his predecessors so it had historical significance. Certainly it was powerful enough to read the message across the square.

DESTROY YOUR COMPUTERS, it said, END THE SCORPION DEATH GRIP. RETURN TO YOUR HOMES AND OFFICE BUILDINGS. DESTROY YOUR COMPUTERS NOW BEFORE THEY DESTROY YOU . . . Suddenly the door burst open and a slender black clad figure appeared on the threshold. He fired without thinking.

"Zebulon," a familiar voice called out as the Terrorist crumpled.

In a minute he was kneeling beside her and had removed the black mask that showed only her eyes, dimming even while he struggled to stem the flow of blood. "Mara!"

"No time," she whispered, touching his face with her hand. "I told them that I would try to talk to you," she gasped.

"Don't," he begged, "save your strength."

She shook her head. "Doesn't matter. If my blood pressure drops that's a signal."

"A signal?"

Her lips formed something resembling a smile. "I came here to talk you into activating the antidote program."

"There is no—"

"Sssh, no time." She covered his mouth with her hand. "When my blood pressure drops, that's the signal."

"But there is no antidote program. The Council of Elders specifically ruled that nothing could turn back the Event."

"Every virus that we planted has a counter virus. Our people did that. The worker bees." She smiled again, then a fit of coughing seized her. "Don't worry," she said, as her eyes began to droop. "Everything's all right. Finally."

The crowd in the Square surged toward the Scorpion Building just as the lights went out. He held her as long as he could. Until the hall outside filled with scuffling and shouting. Until the gunfire sounded outside his door and the building was finally overrun.

TWENTY

When he came to, McAuliffe was loosening the buttons on his shirt, propping him up and forcing a vile smelling liquid down his throat.

"Slipped you the Mickey, they did," a now familiar British voice boomed in his direction.

"Shut up, Lionel," McAuliffe snapped, "bring me the spitoon. Quick, before he starts heaving again."

"Dashed disgusting task for a man of my rank," Sir Lionel Wisdom rolled the huge brass bowl under his chin while McAuliffe held his head. "Should have servants to take care of this," Sir Lionel averted his eyes.

McAuliffe continued to hold on to him, stroking his head. "That's right," he crooned, "get it all out. You'll be fine now."

Christian's eyes streamed with tears as McAuliffe wiped his face and cleaned off the front of his shirt.

"McNamara," he whispered as soon as he caught his breath.

"I know," McAuliffe sighed and propped him against the settee. "Poor Mac. He's going to be your roommate for just a little while longer. This gives us the evidence we need, you know. Gartner's finally hung himself."

"Jolly good show, youngster." Sir Lionel boomed, patting his back vigorously. "Leading us right to old Mac while we still had time—"

"Time," Christian whispered, "What time?"

"Eleven thirty-five."

"Have to go," he struggled to a sitting position, "before he takes her. Julie."

"Don't worry about Julie. We'll take good care of her. You just rest for a few minutes."

"My friends," President McKinley's voice was calling for order as McAuliffe slipped back into the hall with Sir Lionel Wisdom.

"The time has come to say good bye to the old century." There was a burst of applause. Gartner waited until it had died down. "It has been a time of growth and dominance for our country. Now they tell us that our power is waning, that globalization is the watchword of the new Millennium. Computers have broken down the boundaries of nationalism, boundaries that our American soldiers died to protect. Today we can look forward to a great global network in which brown men, red men and yellow men take their place beside the white. Yes, my friends, that's what they tell us and I say "horsefeathers!"

The room erupted with cheering just as Christian

pulled himself to a standing position and made his way slowly, leaning on walls and furniture, to the edge of the velvet drapes. "Horsefeathers!" he shouted and the crowd went wild for the second time.

"I didn't work all my life to turn everything I own over to a bunch of people who aren't even fit to be my servants. Why, you can't get a decent meal in this country today, can't register in a good hotel, can't pick up a newspaper without some ethnic from a country you never heard of assuring you that it's 'no problema.' My friends, I believe that they are the problema and that history teaches us how to stamp it out!"

"And what about the cab drivers?" The audience was whistling and stamping its feet. "Who are these men, wearing turbans and hanging air freshener on their rear view mirrors, who are these people who can't speak my language telling me to put out my cigarette. Who are they—?"

Christian edged out of the alcove just as the liveried butler who had welcomed them, stepped up to deliver a note to Mr. Gartner. He opened it, read it and smiled. "My associates tell me that there isn't time to recount all the weaknesses of the present economy. Instead we've got to get on to the event that promises to reverse them. My friends," he thundered, his eyes snapping with electricity, "will you join hands with me and ask the Almighty to bless our endeavor?"

The crowd fell silent as Gartner grasped Julie's hand and led her down into their midst. That's it," he said, handing her down to a man in a tight celluloid collar. She seemed to stumble as she stepped off the stairs and into the crowd. "Now join hands with Mrs. McKinley and me and let's petition the Lord in the words that He himself taught us. Our Father," he began and the crowd mumbled along after him, "Which art in heaven, hallowed be . . ."

Christian joined the circle, managing to slip between Julie and the distinguished white haired woman to her right. "Julie," he leaned down to whisper in her ear but she didn't seem to recognize him. Her eyes were large and vacant. "Julie," he whispered more urgently, "it's Christian."

Gartner had reached a thunderous Amen and bowed his head. "Christian," she cried into the silence, happy at last to see him, even though her smile was a little vague.

Gartner's head shot up. "Christian? Son, is that you? Why don't you step up here and join us?"

Two men in celluloid collars grabbed him from behind and strong-armed him up the stairs. Maybe they were policemen, keeping their cover until the last second. Please God, let them be policemen.

"Christian?" Julie trailed along after them.

"There now, easy does it." Gartner chided his associates as they delivered him stumbling up the stairs to the landing.

"Well, son, you're just in time for our little ceremony, you and your degenerate friends. Step up here so that we can all see the best this century has to offer." Hoarse laughter erupted from the men in the audience. The women tittered behind their hands. Some of them looked away, obviously pained by the display of vulgarity.

"That's far enough, Gartner." McAuliffe's voice

rang out from the back of the room. "Your little game is over. Lionel, please relieve Mr. McKinley and his associates of their weapons."

There was a long pause during which the grin on Gartner's face grew broader. "No answer? Perhaps he can't hear you. Gentlemen, why don't you take Mr. McAuliffe upstairs so that he can join the rest of his friends."

There was a scuffle and shots broke out in the back of the room. Gartner reached for his own gun just as Christian rushed him. He could hear Julie's screams as they scuffled, then the gun went off and Gartner's body went slack with surprise.

"No!" he flung Christian aside and raced to Julie's side. "No!"

Gartner cradled her gently in his arms. "No," he sobbed, "no." Blood was bubbling from her mouth.

An elderly white haired gentleman fought his way up through the crowd. "Make way," someone called, "it's Dr. Pierce."

Gartner laid her down gently as the Doctor bent to his work. Then he picked up his pistol. "Save her," he aimed at the old man's head.

Dr. Pierce flashed him a look of disdain. "Save your theatrics for the underlings, Hieronymous. I'm already half dead so there's no use making any threats. As for this child here," he fumbled for Julie's pulse. "She's in shock and there's nothing going to save her but an ambulance and an operation. Both of which are scheduled to disappear from the face of the earth," he consulted his watch, "within the next five minutes."

Gartner stood with both hands gripping the butt of the pistol, waving it back and forth. Who should he shoot? Who was responsible? His gaze lighted on Christian and the pistol steadied.

"So what's it going to be, man," Dr. Pierce continued in his matter-of-fact voice, "Are we going back in time or do you want me to save this young lady's life?"

Christian closed his eyes, certain that Gartner would fire.

When he opened them, the man was shaking. "Activate the antidote program," he barked.

Christian looked around.

"You!" Gartner shrieked. "This is no time to play dumb. Activate the program."

"What program?"

"The antidote! The one your mother asked about. I told her that the virus couldn't be stopped and she laughed. She told me that she would ask her son. He worked for the Doomsday Group. He was their star programmer. He knew all about it."

"And you believed her?"

"Don't lie to me," he shrieked, "You corrupted my program, you and that idiot Slater—."

Christian shook his head. "No," he said, his face streaming with tears, "no, I didn't. I wish I had." A strange rattling sound came from Julie's throat.

The grandfather clock began to chime. 1, 2, 3 . . . The people in the hall were clinging to each other. Men sobbing. Women with their faces buried against their husband's chests. A woman began to moan. At the stroke of twelve, the room fell into silence. Cheering could be heard clearly from the street and the sound of fireworks.

"What time is it?" Gartner rasped.

The liveried butler consulted the digital watch he still wore concealed under his sleeve. "12:03, a.m., Sir."

"And the date, man, tell me the date?"

"January 1, Sir, in the year 2000."

Hieronymous Gartner turned the gun on himself.

TWENTY ONE

ernard McAuliffe was buried as a detective. The promotion came through on the day that he died of gunshot wounds in Northwestern Hospital. Lena went with Christian to the Mass. McAuliffe's brothers sat in the front of the church with their families. They were tall, raw-boned men whose eyes flicked anxiously from side to side, making them appear furtive and ashamed of their grief.

No one could believe what had happened. Not the companies whose programs failed, nor the people who read the story in the newspapers and watched it on television. Not even the bereaved. So many rich and famous men, the heads of companies and governments. Surely they could not all be taken in by the same outlandish plot. There must be something they're not telling us, everyone said. Christian thought the publicity would be good for his mother's book.

"The paper said there were people all over the world, all dressed up, sitting in old houses, waiting to go back in time." Lena reached for her cigarette and took a deep drag, studying the smoke thoughtfully as it rose above their heads. The funeral was over and they were sitting in the Greek's having breakfast.

"On Mackinac Island they just took for granted it had happened. They're so isolated, you know, with the horses and all. It wasn't till the mail boat arrived they realized that something was wrong. There they were, prancing around, all dressed up and in comes the motorized mail boat." She stubbed out her cigarette. "Bet they felt like a bunch of fools." She gave a deep phlegmy chuckle that quickly turned into a cough.

Christian dipped his toast in the egg.

"And your poor mother gone, for nothing, for a made up story, a crazy idea in a rich man's head."

He ate for a while in silence. "Lena, remember that picture I told you about, the one Tess had in her desk?"

Lena was sorting through her purse, counting out dollars for the tip. She looked up briefly and nodded.

"Well, I found it. I thought it had been stolen, that it was part of a cover up. It turns out it was there all the time, it had just fallen behind the drawer. Here, take a look."

Lena put on her glasses and studied the boy with his shirt off, squinting into the sun. "My God," she said finally, putting her hand in front of her mouth. "We were so young, all of us." Her eyes had filled with tears.

"Can you tell who it is?" Christian's heart hammered in his chest. "Can you tell me if he's my father?"

"Oh Lamb," she opened her arms and Christian slid across the vinyl bench. "They're all your father, all of them boys who died before they became men, before they could see their sons, all of them, praying for you, hoping you'll do well, that you'll live longer and better than they did. That your life will give theirs some meaning."

"But who is he? This particular boy and why did she keep his picture?"

"Lord, I don't know. Why did she do anything the way she did?"

"You don't know who he is?"

"That's poor Skinny Mulligan, died of a burst appendix waiting for a helicopter to take him out of the jungle."

"And what was his real name?"

Lena frowned, reaching back in her memory. "Frank," she said finally, "I think his name was Frank."

The full extent of the conspiracy will never be known nor how much time has been lost. Teams of scientists were assembled to trace its roots and it is from their reports that we know as much as we do. But ultimately the task of understanding was set aside and all our energies focused on the larger task of going forward. It is human nature to cling to the past, after all, and to imagine that we see in it the mirror of our future.

The truth is that we will never understand our own lives, no matter how hard we try. The passing of the Millennium reminds us that there are patterns larger than our vision. Our worth is measured on a scale that is longer than our own lifespan, larger than our reason. All around us nature is decomposing, enriching the soil and giving birth to new life. We cannot open our eyes without seeing the cycle of life, death, regeneration and change repeated everywhere we look. Yet we claim not to understand.

We must love ourselves, every molecule, every breath, and give our blessing to whatever task falls on our generation, no matter how great or small. We must trust that our lives will combine with others to yield worlds that we cannot imagine, sons and daughters that we would not recognize but who are nevertheless our true heirs.